DIVINITY

PATRICIA LEEVER

OMNIFIC PUBLISHING

DALLAS

Divinity, Copyright © 2012 by Patricia Leever
All Rights Reserved. Except as permitted under the U.S. Copyright Act of 1976,
no part of this publication may be reproduced, distributed, or transmitted
in any form or by any means, or stored in a database or retrieval system,
without prior written permission of the publisher.

Omnific Publishing
10000 North Central Expressway, Dallas, TX 75231
www.omnificpublishing.com

First Omnific eBook edition, September 2012
First Omnific trade paperback edition, September 2012

The characters and events in this book are fictitious.
Any similarity to real persons, living or dead,
is coincidental and not intended by the author.

Library of Congress Cataloguing-in-Publication Data

Leever, Patricia.
  Divinity / Patricia Leever – 1st ed.
  ISBN 978-1-62342-907-2
  1. Supernatural — Romance. 2. Fantasy — Romance.
  3. Hollywood — Romance. 4. Magic/Occult — Fiction. I. Title

10 9 8 7 6 5 4 3 2 1

Cover Design by Micha Stone and Amy Brokaw
Interior Book Design by Coreen Montagna

Printed in the United States of America

“I do not suffer from insanity, I enjoy every minute of it.”
~ Edgar Allen Poe

CHAPTER 1
EVELYN

Demons.

They're everywhere, hiding in plain sight. Lawyers, doctors, politicians, the guy on the corner, the lady ringing up your groceries, your kid's principal, or the over-exuberant PTA mom who runs every bake sale and fundraiser at the school.

Chances are, you've interacted with one or two of them in your lifetime without even realizing it on a conscious level. But your body knew.

Deep down in your bones, you sensed something wrong and unholy about them. There was something in the cut of their jib that just made your skin crawl and set your teeth on edge, a natural, innate reaction to their unnaturalness. Instinct.

My name is Evelyn Elizabeth Brighton. I work for the Lebriga Corporation. And I hunt demons.

If you were to see me on the street, I would look like any other twenty-three-year-old, give or take a year or two. And once upon a time, I was.

As I stood in the shower, the warm water beat down on the back of my neck, spilling over my shoulders and loosening up the muscles coiled tight under my skin. I'd been on countless assignments over the years, but I still tensed up every time like it was the first one.

That's the way I liked it, though; it kept me fresh and on my toes. My point of view was if I ever came to a point of complacency, I deserved to have my ass handed to me by whatever beast I happened to be wrestling with at the time.

Today I was in a run-down, nasty motel in the shittiest part of Los Angeles, preparing for the next assignment: a Moriscon demon, a particularly slimy breed that prided itself on the art of manipulation. They were used-car salesmen, talent scouts, and the like. Back in the day, they traveled from town to town peddling tonics and elixirs and inevitably running off with the pretty young farm girl who was never to be heard from again. They were smooth talkers, song-and-dance men.

Moriscon usually worked with two or three lesser creatures, generally trolls, because they were easy to control and to disguise, not unlike the demons themselves.

This demon in particular had a photography studio with pictures of well-known young actresses displayed in the window, two goons on staff, and a penchant for naïve, straight-off-the-bus-from-Kansas, nubile young girls. Luckily, I played dumb, wide-eyed country girl really, really well.

As I stepped out of the bathroom, my cell phone chirped with a text message notice:

Hey E, it's a go. Don't get dead. ~T

T, Tessa, was my handler. She made sure I knew where to go, when to go, and that I had everything I needed to get the job done. She was also my best friend and had wicked-accurate gut instincts, something that came in quite handy in our line of work.

I wrapped the chintzy hotel towel over my hair, twisted it into a turban, and threw on my clothes. Sitting in the middle of the bed, I picked through my bag of tricks, the tools of the trade: blades, guns, and lots of ammo. Each and every piece of metal had been consecrated by the high mucky-mucks at Lebriga.

This assignment was also going to call for me to work some serious magic to get the job done, and not just the usual scent-masking charm either. Because this nasty Mo liked his meat young, it called for a pretty hefty age spell.

As I plucked the small white envelope out of the assignment-order packet Tess had tucked into my backpack, I tested the weight in my hand. I could see that it was thicker and heavier than normal, and I knew what that meant. The more powder used, the younger the result. Man alive, I was really going to enjoy sending this putrid sack of pseudo-human flesh back to the hell, or whatever dimension, he had slithered out of.

Rifling through my bag, I pulled out my casting pot and black candle and set them on the rickety table in the corner of the room. I strapped my sword to my back and slung on my jacket, concealing my baby. She was one wicked piece of cold hard steel encased in charmed leather that made her pliable, able to conform to my body as I moved. But as soon as she was free, she sang with immense power.

After tying a dagger to my ankle, I braided my hair and tugged on a blond wig, stuffing any loose strands underneath. At the table, I poured the powder into the bowl and lit the candle as I began to recite the incantation I'd spoken so many times before:

G'ea anst'd n'wod
Toh'uy sire veabo.

I said this three times and touched the candle to the powder with a quick flash of blue light and a puff of purple smoke.

Now for the weird part.

I closed my eyes and felt my skin tingle as the magic settled in and covered my exposed flesh. Slowly lifting one lid, I peeked at myself in the mirror and was taken aback by what stared back at me. I looked like I was fifteen, if that. I almost lost my lunch when I thought about all the young girls who it was too late for.

Maintain, Evie. You need to stay calm or you're going to break the spell before you even leave the room.

Strolling out of the motel, I headed down the street, flinging my backpack over my shoulder as I walked toward the location. This place was supposed to be "off Sunset Boulevard"; apparently, that meant three blocks east and four blocks south of it. As I rounded the last corner, I saw my destination:

DICK STARR PHOTOGRAPHY
LET US MAKE YOU A STAR

I think I'm going to hurl.

Dickey Slick's little studio was a boil on the ass of this city. Well, one of them anyway.

I checked my reflection in the window of a nearby store to make sure the spell was holding. So far, so good. As long as it held long enough for me to get in the door and make sure there weren't any innocents in there with this sick bastard, I was on point.

A series of tinkling bells announced my arrival as I opened the door.

"I'll be right there," a vaguely female voice called from the back office, and I heard the very distinct plop of slimy troll feet hitting linoleum as the creature made its way to the front of the shop where I was. I knew to the untrained ear it sounded like the normal canter of human footfall, but I'd always had the ability to see what others couldn't or wouldn't see. That's one of the reasons why I did this. One can't deny one's natural, God-given talent.

"Hi, what can I do for you today?" She surveyed my appearance, probably trying to pick up on my scent. Trolls had a keen sense of smell and fancied themselves as being able to sniff out a hunter from ten miles away. Luckily, they weren't the brightest beings in the creature world and were easily fooled with a simple masking incantation. "Hang on…let me guess…portfolio package, right?"

Perfect, the magic is doing its job. I'm in. Time to throw out the line and see if the fish are biting today.

"Oh my gosh, how did you know?" I asked, using my most sickeningly sweet voice. God, I hated that voice.

"Because you, sweetie, look like the next big thing." Her grizzled green lips curled over her yellow teeth in what I'm sure appeared to be a sweet smile, but I saw under the façade, and it was all I could do not to shudder at the sheer grossness before me. "I'm going to be honest with you, though, hon'. You look pretty young, and if you're under eighteen, we're going to need your parents to sign a release."

"Oh," I said, putting on my best dejected, sad-puppy face, hoping she'd take the bait. "Well, my parents really don't know I'm here." I threw in one of those uncertain bottom lip bites for good measure.

"Hmm, they really need to be here with you, sweetie, I'm sorry. Hey, why don't you come back with one of them a little later this afternoon, and we can see what we can do about turning you into a star. How about that?"

This racket was smarter than I thought, but luckily I was smarter. I knew what this feigned concern really was—they were covering their ass. If they were going around snacking on the local fodder, it would raise eyebrows; missing child reports would start to pop up, and the next thing they knew, cops would be breathing down their necks.

"Um, they don't exactly live around here," I said, shoving my hands into my pockets and working the toe of my sneaker against the linoleum.

Her greasy green skin vibrated with excitement; this was precisely what she wanted to hear.

"Where do they live, honey?"

Ugh, one of her stomachs just rumbled.

"Little River, Kansas." I juggled my backpack in front of me as I unzipped the front pocket. "But I have money. I can pay you right now, in cash."

I swear to God, I could practically see her salivate when she spied the Greyhound bus tag tied to my bag. Tess really had thought of everything.

"Stop right there…don't move, and just stay exactly where you are," I heard from behind me.

A "man" walked around in front of me, looking me up and down—probably trying to decide how he would carve me up, which parts he wanted to keep for himself and which ones to throw to his two goons. It was weird how I saw demons and the like. I could see beneath the opaque outer shell that most everyone saw, a smokescreen of sorts over their true selves.

He reached out a gnarled gray claw to me. "I'm Dick, and I am going to make you one of my stars."

My pre-assignment burger was halfway up my throat at the serious line of bullshit this guy was slinging. Did people really buy this crock? His black veins pulsed under the thin veil of demon skin on the back of his hand as he held it out for me to shake.

Ick. I really didn't want to touch it, not with my bare hand, anyway. Part of me wanted to yank my sword off my back and just whack the hunk of flesh off at the wrist. But there was still a troll missing, and I needed all three of them in the same room to lessen the chance of someone escaping and me having to hunt them down. Not that hunting wasn't fun; sometimes I enjoyed a good chase. But I wasn't in the mood for running through the back alleys of Los Angeles. I just wanted to get this over with and get the hell out of there.

I reached out, hoping that the spell would hold if I made physical contact with the evil beast. We'd just about connected when Smelly Troll Number Two came stumbling out of the back room. Really, this thing reeked so badly that I highly doubted whatever black magic was being used to disguise that joker was enough to hold the stench back.

"Sir…uh, I mean, Dick, the table…err…the studio is ready."

About that time, Slick Dick's sharp eye caught the hint of the tattoo on the inside of my wrist.

"What's this now," he said, grappling my hand and yanking my sleeve up my arm.

As soon as his unnatural flesh touched my skin, I could feel the magic of the age incantation dissolving. It was irrelevant at that point, though; the ink wrapped around my wrist was in full view. I looked up and saw his beady red eyes staring down at me, and his top lip twitched up angrily.

I was made.

Stink Boy pointed a fat sausage finger at me from across the room. "HUNTER!" he yelled — screamed like some otherworldly little girl was more like it.

Biting down on the holy water gel capsule I'd tucked into my cheek just before walking in, I spat in Tricky Dick's eye.

With an ear-piercing screech that only demons were capable of, he turned me loose and scrubbed at what I knew was an incessant burning in his eyes.

Spinning out from under him, I quickly reached into my backpack, whipped out my semiautomatic handgun, and gave Stinky a bullet right between the eyes, just to shut him the hell up. I flung my jacket off and shoved the gun in the back of my pants as I pulled my sword off my back. This blade had been good to me over the years, and together we'd relieved many a demon of their heads.

I swung at Demon Dick, and the rat bastard dodged, taking a swipe at me as he vaulted to the ceiling. He clung to the paneling like a giant bat as he growled and hissed orders to the she-troll in Morisconic, his born language. The next thing I knew, his slimy Girl Friday was hurling herself in my direction. One thing about trolls was, even though they might not have been the brightest bulbs in the box, they were impossibly strong.

She gnashed her crooked, bile-colored teeth, excreting and building the amount of viscous, green saliva in her mouth. It spilled over her lips in strings, dangling and swaying in her wiry chin hair. Trolls also tended to bite and had the most disease-ridden, disgusting pie holes in the neighboring dimensions and every level of Hell combined.

I ducked down, rolled on one shoulder, and leapt to my feet behind Miss Big Green and Gross. Taking a deep breath, I jumped onto her back and wrestled my arm around the front of her thick neck. Damn but it was hard getting a good grip amidst the sludge her body secreted out of its giant pores, and then there was the smell — it was beyond rank.

"You seriously reek. You know that, right?" My grasp slipped and slid in creature goop as I reached down for the dagger strapped to my ankle. I really didn't want to get this thing's blood on me because the stench was gag-inducing and stayed on you for a good week.

With one quick tug, I sliced right through the giant carotid artery, or whatever it was called in this species, and sprang back off of her, trying to avoid the arterial spray. Sally Slime Bucket slid to the floor, gurgling and sputtering into a dark green pool of putrid troll juice.

I heard the clicking and scratching overhead as the main attraction skittered across the ceiling.

I hate to say it, but as sick and twisted as it sounds, I loved this part. I pulled off the blond wig and threw it to the ground as my own chestnut-brown braid slid down my back. Tugging my long-sleeved T-shirt over my head, I revealed the dozens of incantations I carried, potent spells tattooed and branded right onto my skin. One of them was so ancient and powerful that it had to be carved into my flesh deep enough to leave a raised white scar.

The Hell spawn muttered a bunch of things in his unholy tongue, but one word that didn't need to be translated was "No."

I drew the tip of my sword across my palm, drawing blood; that part was important. My blade was powerful and deadly in her own right, but coupled with the blood from a single, self-inflicted wound? We were downright unstoppable, and the beast knew it because he began pleading for his life.

That was step one. There seemed to be a general order in which these types of things happened; it must have been in the demon handbook or something.

"Look, Dickless, can we just cut to step three? I mean we both know how this is going to go down, right? You've already started with the begging. You *know* I'm not gonna buy any of your crates of crap, so save it. Then you're gonna try to run. I don't know why, because you *know* I can't let you leave. So can we just cut to the fighting so I can kill you and get it over with?" I asked. "Get your greasy gray ass down here and fight me like a man, bitch. Come on."

He looked at me for a second like he wasn't sure I'd really just said all that, then his hind legs twitched, and I knew he was going to make a run for it.

Shit.

I spoke the sealing spell and sealed all of the doors and windows—no one could get in, and no one could get out. This incantation in particular was some serious magic because this sucker stuck until it was released.

The demon knew those words, knew what the spell meant, and knew that if he killed me he'd be stuck in there forever. Finally, with a very intimidating growl, he dropped to his feet on the other side of the studio.

My skin prickled with excitement, and I positively pulsated with the power of the incantations. This was the moment I lived and breathed for, and I couldn't stop the grin that spread over my face. This is what I was born to do.

The creature held out one of his arms and started to carve through it with a black talon. What the hell was he doing?

Reaching in, he probed, and I could see his two fingers moving under the thin skin. There was snapping and crunching before this dude slowly pulled one of his arm bones out to wield as a weapon. This was new.

"Oh, see? Now that is just wrong," I said just before he charged me.

My blade collided with the bone he'd fished out of his body; it didn't splinter like normal calcified matter would. But then again, this situation wasn't even in the realm of normal anymore.

He blocked and countered every move I made as we moved and danced in the heat of battle. Suddenly, I felt a pull inside of me, a familiar tug on my insides that told me I was missing something. I quickly glanced around the room as our weapons clashed and saw the door that Stinky had come out of.

That's when his words clicked in my memory: "*Sir, the table is ready.*"

Holy shit, there's an innocent here, behind that door.

Pushing the demon back with my last advance, I felt the power of the magic moving through me, the warmth of the incantations as they worked to give me strength. With every lunge, I was stronger and more pissed off.

He spat curses at me, trying to distract me as we moved deeper into the studio, closer to the back door, and every step increased the pull on my gut and the rage surging through my veins. I swung again, shouting the spell of strength, and I felt the magic vibrate up my body, into my arms, and radiate out of my blade. His crude weapon shattered like glass, exploding on impact and rendering him unarmed.

"Please, please…" he pled, his hands covering his face as he backed up against the big green door in the rear.

I swung my blade back. She glowed with magic, and I could feel her intense need to finish this. Using all of my might, I buried my sword up to the hilt into the demon's gut, pinning him to the door. Black blood flooded out around my hands as I twisted my weapon and recited the final words:

"With my sword, I damn you and send you back to Hell. May the pain of every innocent soul you've stolen come back on you tenfold until the end of time." As I pulled my blade free, the useless shell of his body slumped to the ground. Seething with rage and magic, I pushed his lifeless body aside and broke down the door.

There, bound by her wrists and ankles and surrounded by plates and carving knives, was a young girl. Her eyes were wide with fear as she took in my appearance and struggled in her restraints. My tattoos and scars cast a pulsing glow, and the fact that I was covered in demon blood to boot couldn't have helped matters; the poor girl was terrified of me.

"It's okay, I'm not going to hurt you," I said as I laid down my sword, slowly approached her, and untied the leather gag in her mouth. "What's your name?"

"A-Amber," she croaked, her body trembling.

"Okay, Amber, let's get you off of this table, okay?"

I worked the straps off of her, and for a split second I saw a familiar look in her eye, one that said she was going to try to deck me. Something told me that this one didn't go quietly and fought with every ounce of her being. I'd bet money that she'd definitely left an impression on her captors, which was why they'd been going for the living feast. Good for her.

As my arms closed around her, she crumbled, sobbing while I helped her to her feet. This was all to be expected; she'd been nearly eaten alive by creatures she probably hadn't known existed until that day.

I steadied her, and we walked out of the twisted banquet hall. We passed the dead demon, and Amber kicked and spat at him. She reminded me of myself, strong with some serious spunk. She and I were going to be working together sometime in the future, I could feel it in my gut.

After I lifted the sealing spell, the Lebriga cleanup crew filed in, complete with the necessary psych personnel to ensure Amber would be okay.

Gotta love Tess and her foresight.

Pulling a fresh shirt out of my backpack, I slipped it on. While walking around downtown LA wearing just a modified sports bra and covered in tats might not raise many an eyebrow, the fact that the incantations still glowed with magic just might.

I fished my phone out of my front pocket and tapped out a text to Tess:

Still kickin & pulled one out of the fire. ~E

Sweet! I knew u would. ~T

Have a gut feeling, did ya? ~E

Haha smart ass. Sbux? ~T

C u in 5. ~E

Shoving my phone back into my pocket, I slung my backpack over my shoulder and walked down the street, getting lost in the hustle and bustle of modern-day Los Angeles. As I stepped onto Santa Monica Boulevard and waited for Tess to pick me up, I watched the happily clueless people go on about their day, oblivious to what had taken place just around the corner.

But that's what we were there for, to keep the peace.

CHAPTER 2
EVELYN

The sudden, annoyingly loud beeping of the alarm jolted me awake. After cursing Tess for buying me that damn clock, I sat up and rolled my neck a few times before I pulled myself out of bed, bent backward, and cracked my back.

Ahhh. That was better.

Padding into the bathroom, I inspected myself in the mirror, then headed into the shower. The ink in my tattoos still had a faint glow, but it would be back to normal the next day, so until then, I was housebound.

To the outside world, our headquarters looked like any another mansion off Mulholland. But underneath the roof of that nondescript estate beat the heart of the Los Angeles branch of the Lebriga Corporation, home to four hunter and handler pairs including Tess and myself, each with our unique specialties.

Hunters did the dirty work: they went out in the field and took care of business working alone or with a partner, depending on the assignment. Our handlers, conversely, worked behind the scenes, making sure we had every ounce of pertinent information for any particular task.

We were matched on a level that went beyond coworkers, friends, or even siblings; what a hunter and a handler had between them was thicker than blood and stronger than the trunk of any family tree. This was the reason that hunters were always paired with same-sex handlers — it kept funny business between the two to a minimum. In fact, it was strictly forbidden for a hunter to even "hook up" with someone else's handler, of either sex. According to the bigwigs overseas, adding sex into the mix would be too much for anyone to handle, mentally and emotionally. The bond was just *that* tight.

But corporate wasn't ignorant and knew that, as humans, we had needs, so it condoned fraternization within our own ranks, without a care as to what our personal sexual preference was. A fact that many took advantage of, except for me — I was just fine on my own. I didn't need anyone else inside my head, messing with my emotions and throwing me off my game.

Besides, being a hunter was dangerous business. I'd seen firsthand what could happen to a hunter who was broken down by loss, and that wasn't going to happen to me, ever.

As I was drying off, my bedroom door burst open.

"Hey, Josie, are you ready to — "

"Jesus, Tony, knock much? She's not in here," I said, trying to cover myself with my towel.

"Sorry," he said with a huge grin as he backed out of the room. Before closing the door behind him, he added, "Nice glow, by the way. It's hot."

Somebody really needed to put him on a leash.

Anthony was in the hunter half of our geek squad. He and his handler, Walter, kept us up to speed on the latest and greatest tech known to man and some that was beyond anything anyone had even dreamed of coming up with yet. At first glance, you would think Tony was the type of guy that needed directions on how to unscrew the lid off a mayonnaise jar. Two hundred eighty pounds of solid muscle covered his six-foot-five-inch frame. A nerd in meathead's clothing. Walter, on the other hand, more than made up for that. Homeboy was one-hundred-percent-pure, Grade-A geek. Complete with inhaler and about twelve different prescriptions for his extensive allergies.

In truth, I liked working with Tony. He was the guy you could always count on to have your back no matter what. His only downfall was my roommate, Josephine. But then again, Josie was a lot of people's downfall.

My door flew open again, slamming against the wall behind it.

"Evie, babe, you comin' down to eat?"

"For crap sake, do closed doors mean nothing in this place?" I yelled, wrestling my towel around myself.

"Geez, someone got up on the wrong side of the bed this morning," the hulking figure said as he ducked in, closing the door behind him.

"Get out, Zach, I need to get dressed," I said, cinching my towel tighter under my arms.

"Aw, come on, it's not like I haven't seen you naked before, Ev." He smiled widely and waggled his dark eyebrows as he walked toward me.

A one-night mistake a few years ago that never seems to stop coming back to bite me in the ass.

"And like I've told you a thousand times, that will *never* happen again."

"You mean to tell me you don't ever think about it? Even when you're all alone at night?" he asked, still walking slowly across the room with a smarmy grin on his face, running his large hand down his chest.

"No, I don't," I growled, feeling the rage building inside me. The ink of my tattoos tingled with it and burned brighter on my skin.

Zach stopped where he was and put his hands up in surrender. "Relax, Evie, I was just messing with you. I didn't mean to piss you off," he said as he slunk out of the room.

Zachary was a nice guy and all; he just didn't know when to quit or when to shut up. He was a loose cannon in the field too, seldom waiting for backup and instead jumping into a situation balls to the wall. Not to mention he kissed like a Saint Bernard: all tongue and drool. He did know his varmints, though. If one slithered up out of the underworld, he and his handler, Finn, knew what made it tick and, more importantly, how to kill it.

After getting dressed, I stepped into the hallway to find Tess headed in my direction.

"Oh good, I was just gonna come get you," she said, bounding over to my side and looping her arm through mine.

Tess and I handled incantations and charms. It was our job to make sure the hunters had what they needed to conjure magic, incorporated into tattoos and brands. Everyone who went out into the field was marked with the most basic elements: protection, strength, and clarity. We had been together longer than any other team in the house, and we knew each other almost as well as we knew ourselves, which was why I recognized that look on her face. The one she got when she was playing matchmaker again. As much as I loved Tessa, I was going to strangle her if she tried to set me up with some random guy in another house again. She always wanted to pair me with the hunter of whatever handler she happened to be diddling with at the time.

"I don't care how 'dreamy' he is, Tess, I'm not interested," I said before she could even start in.

"For your information, I was not going to try to set you up again," Tessa said with a huff as she planted her feet, jerking me to stop.

"Good, 'cause I'm hungry." I gave her a good tug to get her moving again.

The smell of bacon and fresh coffee greeted me as we hit the last step and turned into the kitchen.

"There you are," Isolde said, her dark blond hair tied into a knot behind her head. She smiled and slid an omelet onto a plate for me.

Isolde was our keeper, our Mama Bear, if you will. She looked after each and every one of us as if we were her own children. "You need to hurry and eat. Alexander wants to see you downstairs. He has another assignment for you."

"Another one?" I asked around the hearty bite of omelet I'd just shoved in my mouth. That was highly unusual. Back-to-back assignments were almost unheard of, especially so close together.

"Less talking, more eating," Tessa said as she bounced in the chair next to me.

"What is with you?" I took a gulp of coffee. "I haven't seen you so excited about an assignment in—"

"Evelyn, in my office, please," squawked Alexander's voice through the intercom system that ran throughout the house.

I stuffed the last bite of omelet into my mouth and hopped out of my chair. "On my way," I said into the box as I pressed the button. Leaning around Isolde, I plucked a freshly baked cheese Danish off the plate. "Thanks for breakfast," I whispered, dropping a peck onto her upturned cheek.

By the time I made it down the stairs and onto the underground level, Tess was already perched on a chair in our shop, thumbing through an ancient book of incantations and taking furious notes. But something wasn't right. Tessa was a fairly excitable person on any given day, but as she sat there she seemed like she was about to come out of her skin.

"What is with you today?" I asked, poking my head into the shop on my way to Alex's office.

Before she could answer, movement at the other side of the corridor caught my eye. I looked down the hall and saw all six feet, three inches of dark-haired, green-eyed hunk of yum wrapped in a tight gray T-shirt, heading my way.

"Ladies." He nodded to us as he passed by, ducking into the weapons room. His voice had a lilt to it that made my knees wobble.

"Who was that?" I asked as I picked my jaw up off the floor.

"That is the new handler," Tess answered, popping up behind me to ogle the new guy.

New handler?

I opened my mouth to ask what the hell was going on when the voice of our fearless leader grabbed my attention.

"Evelyn, today, please," he said as he leaned out of his office door. That was Alexander-speak for, "Get your raggedy ass in here, right now."

Alexander was the boss man. He had the direct line to Lebriga's main office overseas. All assignments and orders went through him, and he doled them out as he saw fit. As far as we all were concerned, his word was law. He was the epitome of class, distinguished with his nice, crisp shirt, tie, and vest — always a vest.

As I rounded the corner into his office, cramming the last piece of cheese Danish into my mouth, I saw that we weren't alone. Leaning against the back wall behind Alex's desk was what I assumed was the other half of Hot Handler Guy from the hallway.

He was leaner but not scrawny by any means. His brown hair was perfectly un-perfect, and a light dusting of scruff swept across his jaw. A mischievously crooked grin spread across his face as his piercing blue eyes blatantly rolled up and down my body.

"Come in and have a seat, Evelyn," Alex said from behind the massive mahogany desk, the tips of his fingers pressed together in thought.

Crap. I had the feeling I was about to hear something I didn't want to.

Alexander and I had worked together for a long time, going back to when we were working out of an abandoned church downtown and Tess and I had been the only crew to speak of. Over the years, a lot of pairs had filtered through our doors, and some of them stuck—like the crew we had now—and some had moved along to another branch, so having a new team in the crew wasn't exactly something out of the ordinary.

What was out of the ordinary was this, right here in Alex's office, this one-on-one bullshit. In the past, newbies were always introduced as a team to the entire crew.

"I'll stand, thank you," I said, my eyebrow quirking up at Alexander as I crossed my arms over my chest. I probably sounded a tad too snarky, but I couldn't help it. This scenario reeked of bad news.

"Very well," Alex said, pushing himself to his feet and crossing to the front of his desk, where he leaned back against it. "I assume you met Christopher, our new handler, out in the hallway, and this is Daniel. He is our newest hunter." He motioned to the prick on the other side of the room.

"Pleasure," Daniel said with that annoying lopsided smirk and a nod in my direction.

"I'm sure it's all yours," I responded with a sickeningly sweet, insincere smile.

Alex took a deep breath and shook his head. "Evelyn, please do not be difficult about this," he said, pinching the bridge of his nose.

"Difficult about what, Alex? I don't even know what 'this' is," I said, waving my hands around to indicate everything in the entire room.

"This is your new assignment. You're to train him to be part of our crew." He spoke in that tone he got when he meant business.

Then it dawned on me where that Christopher guy had been headed when I'd seen him in the hallway: the weapons room. We'd been without weapons specialists for about six months, ever since Frank and Lee had transferred to take the lead position at the Miami branch. I thought we were doing okay, taking care of our own weapons and whatnot. Apparently the higher-ups thought differently.

I stood silently staring at the inkwell on Alex's desk, my teeth working the inside of my bottom lip, trying to figure out some way to get out of this crappy assignment. When nothing came to mind, I had to face facts: this was an order, and I didn't have a choice.

"Fine." I'd do my job, but I didn't have to like it. "Warm up and meet me in the training room in fifteen. I need to see what I have to work with here," I said, directing over my shoulder as I headed out of the office.

While I changed into my workout gear, Josie, one of the other hunters, came in toweling sweat off her forehead. Josephine Mira was tall, drop-dead gorgeous, and had legs that went on for days. But put her behind the wheel of a car and she could blow the doors off any stunt driver in Hollywood. And her handler, Meg, could tweak and coax every ounce of power out of any vehicle; she knew her engines inside-out and backward. Our resident gearheads.

Josie was fine to work with as long as you knew what set her off—like having food anywhere near one of her cars. Some of the other branches referred to her and Meg as "The Bitch Squad." They just didn't know them the way we did, but I could see where the two of them could seem standoffish and, well, bitchy.

"So, I saw the fresh meat in Alexander's office this morning. Very nice," she said, with a suggestive wiggle of her eyebrows.

"He's semi-attractive, I guess, if you're into that kinda thing. He's a little too pretty for me."

"Everybody's a little too something for you, Evie," she said with a shake of her head as she walked into the shower.

What the hell is that supposed to mean?

"She's right, you know," Tess said from the other side of my locker door, startling the crap out of me.

"Jesus, Tess, you know I hate it when you sneak up on me like that. Did you know this was coming?" I propped my foot up on the bench and tied my shoes. "You're my handler, my best friend. If you had one of your gut feelings, you should have warned me."

"And said what? That everything you didn't know you were looking for in a guy would stroll through the office and piss you off? You would have bolted in a hot minute, and don't try to tell me different; you can't lie to me and you know it. The fact of the matter is, when all of this is over, I know you're going to realize that you need him, and I think you know it too because you can feel it already. You can't hunt forever, Ev."

"The hell I can't." I plucked a towel off the hook on the wall. "And I think you need to get your gut checked because it's never been more off-base," I said as I turned and walked out of the locker room.

Daniel was already waiting on the square, padded floor of the training room. His fingers reached down his spine as he stretched his triceps. The muscles in his back rolled under the thin cotton of his T-shirt when he twisted his torso, and the thick tendons of his neck pulled taut as he bent his head to one side then the other, his lips pursing together as he held each stretch.

Maybe this isn't going to be so horribly unpleasant after all. The thought crept into my brain before I could stop it.

"Well, there you are, hon'. Ready to get dirty?"

And then he speaks. Did he just call me "hon"?

With a sweet smile, I sauntered over to where he stood and gently took his hand in mine. Taking his first two fingers in my grip, I bent them back, bringing him to his knees in front of me.

"First things first: if you want to keep the ability to use these two fingers, *never* call me 'hon' again, is that clear?"

"Crystal," he grunted, the corners of his eyes beginning to water.

"Good." I let go and took a few steps back. "Now get up and show me what you can do."

Daniel took two steps toward me, and I immediately knew he was holding back by the way he moved. He was probably afraid to hurt me or some ridiculous crap like that. I knocked him to the ground using the most basic of defense techniques. If he even thought about coming out of an actual assignment alive, he was going to have to step it up.

"Why don't we try that again, and don't hold back this time," I instructed, moving to the other side of the room. "Trust me, *you* aren't going to hurt *me*."

His lip curled up with determination as he came at me, full speed this time. Excellent, he was a fast learner. We rolled on the ground, fighting for the upper hand. With him having nearly a foot and about eighty pounds on me, he gained quickly, and I found myself pinned underneath him with that jackass grinning like he'd just won.

I muttered an incantation under my breath and felt a jolt of strength pulse through my body as I turned the tables on him and pinned him in about three seconds.

"Don't be afraid to use your spells; they're there to help you," I said as my forearm pressed against his throat.

"I was, but nothing is happening," he wheezed, struggling to get out from under my grip.

"Can you feel any tingling, any kind of heat at all?" I climbed off him and held out a hand to help him up.

"No," he said, cracking his neck, "not in my ink, anyway."

I could feel my right eyebrow arch up as I tried to think of what could be wrong. "Take off your shirt. I need to check your markings."

He reached back and tugged the navy blue tee over his head.

Damn.

The back of my neck prickled and heat flooded my system at the sight of his naked chest. As much as I hated to admit it, I wouldn't have complained one bit if Daniel decided to never wear a shirt again. He was muscular and toned with just the right amount of body hair, not the hairless bulk that Tony and Zach carried. No, long and lean — that was Daniel, and he was nothing short of perfect, which only irritated me even more. I didn't need that, not right then and not with him.

I pressed my hands to his skin over the inked lettering above his right pec. Something was off. I should have been able feel any magic if there was any to be felt. Nothing. The tattoo didn't even look like it had been done correctly.

"Turn around," I said, trying to sound aloof. The last thing I needed was this guy thinking I was hot for his body or something like that. I was there to do a job, period. I took a step forward as my eyes swept over the smooth planes of his muscled back. There were two poorly scripted incantations, but not what I was looking for. "Raise your arms," I said, ducking around either side, inspecting every inch of visible flesh until I saw something peeking out from under the waistband of his sweat shorts. I curled my finger around the elastic and eased it down a half an inch. There, just what I was looking for: the hunter's brand. At least whoever had marked him couldn't screw that up.

"You know, I don't think anyone is in my room right now." His voice was smooth and husky, and any other girl in her right mind would have jumped at that opportunity. But I wasn't any other girl, and it didn't matter that the air between us buzzed with some palpable kinetic energy; I had a job to do.

"Give me a break." I shoved his shirt back into his hand. "What branch did you train in?"

"Chris and I were recruited out of college, in Indiana, and sent to a facility in a desert in Nevada to train."

Figures. That was probably the same branch Zach and Finn had come from twelve years earlier, and they'd been just as green. Half of Zach's tattoos had needed to be fixed, and the accents for the incantations they'd taught him were all wrong.

"You need more work than you're probably worth, but we'll see what we can do," I said, swiping the towel across my neck to mop up the sweat pooling there.

"What the hell is that supposed to mean?"

Apparently I'd hit a nerve. As I looked back, I noticed a faint glow under his shirt. The incantation that wrapped around his left shoulder was illuminated; he was pissed. So, maybe there was some potential underneath all the pretty.

"It means we have a lot of work to do. Look, I'm not going to sugarcoat it: you're very raw, and I can't tell yet if you're a diamond in the rough or just a regular lump of coal." I turned to leave. "Get some lunch and meet me in my shop later, and I'll see if I can't fix your ink."

After I changed, I popped back into Alexander's office.

"How's our newest hunter faring?" he asked from behind his computer screen.

"He needs a lot of work," I replied as I plopped into the chair on the other side of his desk.

I could see his silver-blond head bob up and down in agreement. "Yes, indeed he does, as did you when I first got a hold of you." He peeked around the monitor and shot me a wink from behind the wire-rimmed glasses he'd had for ages.

He was right. I'd been quite the piece of work when he'd found me holed up in Agnews, The Great Asylum for the Insane, in northern California. Granted, I wasn't really crazy, but that's where they used to put a person who claimed to see demons walking around masquerading as regular people. If I were smart, I would have kept my mouth shut, but I had always been more outspoken than was proper for a lady in the late nineteenth century. God's honest truth, I probably would have wound up in there anyway for mouthing off because ladies were meant to be fawned over. Ha!

Two years, countless sessions in the back electric-shock room, ice baths, and more drugs than my body should have been able to handle later, Alex and Isolde had shown up. Posing as dementia specialist Klaus von Liechtenstein and his nurse Inga, they had claimed to be from Germany, where schizophrenia was on the cutting edge of psychiatry. After telling the doctors at Agnews that I was to be part of a new study, the hospital had been more than happy to be rid of me; I hadn't exactly been the model patient.

Shortly after Alex and Isolde had saved me, they'd begun to train me as a hunter, and like all born hunters, I'd been a natural. They had soon paired me with a red-haired girl they'd yanked out of an asylum in Atlanta, where she'd been committed for having "premonitions" — Tessa. We'd all been together ever since, hunting and training all over the country.

As the world progressed around us, so had the underworld, cranking out new breeds of demons and other nightmare fodder left and right. The days of getting orders by courier and wire were replaced when the Lebriga Corporation had been formed by the powers that be in the late forties.

"Is there anything else?" Alex asked as he went back to his work.

"Why me? Why not Tony or even Zach? Hell, Daniel came from the same training facility as he did, and Zach would have been able to spot the shoddy work from a mile away. Why am I the lucky one that gets stuck with the noob?"

Alexander stopped typing and shifted in his chair as he pushed the computer monitor aside and carefully took off his Klaus glasses. "Because there is no other hunter better qualified to teach Daniel what he needs to know, and you might find you could learn a thing or two from him as well, Evelyn."

Yeah, well, we'll see about that.

CHAPTER 3
DANIEL

My temples throbbed as my teeth ground together, going over in my head how thoroughly Evelyn had shown me who was in charge. Jesus, she pissed me off. Without even thinking, I balled up my fist and punched my locker door. As the rattling sound of metal echoed off the walls of the locker room, I heard whistling: "Battle Hymn of the Republic." Only one person in this house would whistle that tune — my handler, Chris.

"So, got your ass handed to ya, huh?" Chris asked as he lay back on one of the locker-room benches and flopped his arm over his eyes.

"Screw you, asshole," I grumbled, whipping off my towel and lobbing it at his head.

"Sick, man," he sputtered as he shot up and ripped the wet towel off his face. "My freaking mouth was open."

"What else is new? When is your mouth not open?" I yanked my clothes on, thinking about one of the last things Evelyn had said to me:

"You need more work than you're probably worth…"

Seriously, what the hell was that supposed to mean? She didn't know me or what I could do. I'd been fast-tracked there from Nevada, goddamn it. Why did I even give a shit what she thought, anyway?

Probably because I'd heard the name Evelyn Brighton about a billion and one times since Chris and I had signed on with Lebriga. Or maybe because I couldn't stop thinking about the way the magic in her body had vibrated against mine. Yeah, that had to be it.

"Hello, McFly," Chris said, waving his hands in front of my face. "Did you even hear a word I just said?"

"Huh? Sorry, man, I was…never mind." I shook my head, attempting to shake off what she'd said in the training ring; she was just trying to get under my skin. Harpy.

Hot, sexy, makes-me-want-to-tear-my-own-hair-out harpy.

"Ha, I saw your 'never mind' out in the hallway earlier, and that little handler of hers is a freak on a leash. I'm gonna have to keep my eye on her," he said with a grin. "Anyway, what I was sayin' is that you were a big fish in a little bowl in Nevada, and corporate recognized that, so they moved you to a bigger aquarium where you can swim with the other big fish, where you belong."

"Yeah, in a tank with a damn barracuda that's trying to take my head off every time I turn around." I closed up my locker and clapped him on the shoulder. "But she's not gonna have my balls in her back pocket, that's for sure. Let's go eat; I'm starving."

Chris and I had met two years earlier when he'd strolled into my dorm room at the University of Indianapolis as my new roommate. We'd hit it off right away, like real-life brother-from-another-mother kind of shit, and after lots of beer at a frat party, we'd realized that we both saw things. Weird things. Things you keep to yourself so you don't wind up being *that* guy, the psycho guy everyone avoided. When we'd discovered that we were both recipients of a full scholarship from the same company, the Lebriga Corporation, it hadn't taken a genius to figure out that our pairing was no random act of the U-Indy housing department.

Sure as shit, about a week after our collective epiphany, a recruiter from LC had shown up at our door, and what he'd had to say made a lot of sense, at least to Chris and me. The way he'd explained it, there was an entire community of people like us, born to see what others wouldn't.

From what we'd gathered, the origins of "the company" went farther back than we could ever fathom, and as long as demons and whatnot roamed Earth, so did we. Balance. Yin and yang, tit for tat and all that good mess. The promise was simple: join the company, hunt demons and other netherworld scum, and you'd be set for life. Which was a whole other thing in and of itself. As an asset of Lebriga, you were protected from things like illness, disease, age…about the only thing they couldn't protect you from was getting chewed up and spit out by some Hell spawn.

But they more than made up for that by giving us tools to help keep that from happening: training, magic, and an endless supply of cash and tech at our fingertips. I mean, really, how could we have refused? Fight the good fight and basically live forever? We'd signed our names on the dotted line and were shipped off to Nevada in under a week, and after about six months we'd run that facility, virtually untouchable.

And now we were the new kids, and as much as I hated to admit it, even to myself, not being on top sucked ass. Especially when it was not so much knowing I wasn't on top anymore, as being knocked down and kicked in the gut by a chick with a God complex who was hell bent on proving she was better than me at everything.

Chris and I ate our lunch in the weapons room, combing through the inventory. Every piece was catalogued in the branch's database with an image, a corresponding number, and when it was used last and by whom. There was some really nice stuff in there, but there was some really old stuff too, ancient. The kind of stuff you hear about but never really get to see in real life, like the Divinity blade. No one had been issued one of those in over a hundred years, and one was right there under the same roof as us. We both geeked out a little bit about that.

Weird thing was, it didn't say to whom the blade had been issued. Divinity blades were specific weapons, bonded to one hunter and one hunter only. If I were a betting man, I'd have bet my ass it was Evelyn's. She was rocking some serious ink from what I could see, which told me she'd been around the block a time or two.

We also took note that a lot of the more modern weapons weren't even in-house, which was a shame, really. Whoever was in charge of the locker before we'd gotten there liked to rock it old school. Not that there was anything wrong with that, but with a tech department that cranked out things I'd only seen in sci-fi shows, the two didn't really jibe.

I'd have bet that between our two teams we could whip up some seriously sick shit based on the inventory we had to work with. Come up with some real cutting edge stuff that would blow corporate right out of the water.

We decided to take the initiative and headed out down the hallway and into the tech room. A giant computer touch-screen took up the expanse of nearly an entire wall; a multitude of hard drives hummed and clicked in the background, and the smell of solder filled the air.

There were two figures in lab coats hunched over either side of a long white table, speaking to each other in what sounded like Chinese to me. Smoked curled from their soldering guns as they worked to attach wires to some kind of computer console thing. Chris cleared his throat, and they both looked up, sporting pairs of magnifying glasses on their faces that made their eyes look comically huge, and I started to laugh.

I stopped smiling when the big one stood up and pulled off his glasses to glare at me. He looked like he was a wall of flesh and bone. I gave him a nod.

"S'up? I'm Dan, and this is Chris, my handler. We just rolled in from Nevada." I yanked Chris through the doorway.

The little guy at the table exchanged the magnifying glasses for another pair that were damn near just as magnifying, and the big one shoved his hands into the pockets of his lab coat as he sized us up.

"So, you're the new guy," he said in a deep bass voice, his face breaking out in a wide dimply grin. "I'm Tony." He shook my hand and hooked his thumb over his shoulder at the little guy sucking on an inhaler. "That hot mess is Walter."

Walter waved in between puffs and managed to choke out a nasally "Hi."

"Welcome to the funhouse. I hear you've already gone a round with Evs in the training ring." He chuckled, clapping me on the back. "I wouldn't sweat it too much, man; she's pretty fresh off an assignment, and she could probably kick all of our asses with the amount of magic she's still pulling."

I didn't know whether to feel pissed off that everyone in the house probably knew how my first training session had gone or a little less like an incompetent rookie.

Chris pitched our idea to trick out some of the older weapons on hand, and those two practically salivated at the suggestion.

Yeah, we were going to get along really freaking well.

After we'd arranged a time to have a good sit-down and draw up plans for the new gadgets, I cursed to myself when I saw what time it was. I was supposed to head over to Evelyn's shop right after lunch. Great.

On the way to the shop, I passed by what Tony referred to as "The Creature Cave" and saw Evelyn. She was standing next to a tall dark guy, looking up at a video playing on a monitor on the wall.

"That, right there," she said, pointing to the scene on the screen of a demon wielding an arm bone as a weapon.

"*Oh, see? Now that is just wrong,*" the female voice off-camera said, and I immediately recognized it as hers.

"Hmm," the big dude hummed and nodded as his hand rested against the small of her back. I had a weird pang in my gut, and my jaw clenched until she elbowed him in the rib cage and told him to knock it the hell off.

I will say one thing: she has one hell of a nice ass, my inner voice commented.

"Mmhm," I agreed, not realizing I'd made the sound out loud until everyone turned around and stared at me.

"There you are. Are you finally done dicking around with Tony and actually ready to get to work?" Evelyn asked.

"Just waiting on you and enjoying the view," I shot back with a grin and a wink, the one that usually got me out of trouble with women.

"Whatever, let's go," she said, glaring at me as she pushed past and rushed down the hallway.

I glanced up at the guy left standing in the middle of the room. Holy crap, that guy was bigger than Tony.

"Danny," I said, shoving a hand in his direction.

"Zach," he replied, his enormous mitt encompassing mine and squeezing a little harder than was necessary as he gave me the once-over. "Everyone calls me Z."

So that was the Z who Sampson, the guy who ran the Nevada training branch, had mentioned before.

"I've heard of you. Sampson speaks very highly of you," I said as I shook his hand.

"You're out of the desert, huh?" He released his vice-like grip. "Then you better get your ass in there with Evie so she can fix your ink. Sammy's a great guy, but a shitty tattoo artist." He turned back to the video on the screen, scrutinizing the creature.

As I stepped into the shop, I saw hundreds of shelves that housed a variety of ceramic pots, glass bottles, metal decanters, and old books. There was an open door in the back leading to a small room with a chair in the middle, and I could hear someone rustling around in there; I assumed it was Evelyn.

"Well, don't just stand there mouth-breathing, get in here, take your shirt off, and have a seat so we can get to work."

Charming as usual.

"That's the proper incantation for the strength spell, broken down phonetically," she said as she poured ink into little wells on the counter, nodding to a folded piece of paper in the seat of the big black chair. "Learn it and know it by tomorrow. Sit down," she ordered without even turning around.

"Could you record yourself saying it correctly for me?" I asked, pulling my iPod out of my pocket and getting to the voice-memo screen.

"Excuse me?" she asked in return, looking at me like I'd just asked her to explain quantum physics.

"It's a learning tool. Having the phonetic text is great, but it helps to have an audio to go with it. You want me to learn this shit by tomorrow or what?"

After a little hesitation, she begrudgingly took the iPod and made a quick recording. I couldn't help but feel some satisfaction that she'd conceded.

Seeing her sitting on the stool with her back to me as she prepared her materials, she looked so unassuming and small. Her hair was swept back in a loose braid that hung down to the middle of her back. I could see a flutter of ink between the bottom of her shirt and the top of her jeans as she leaned forward. My brain spun with wonder at what could be etched into her skin and how I could go about finding out for myself.

I pulled my shirt over my head and tossed it into the corner—that's when I spotted the sword on the wall.

Sweet hell, a Divinity blade. Right there in the same freaking room. I wanted to touch it so badly but knew better. Touching it would knock me on my ass in a hot minute. The only way anyone could lay hands on a Divinity blade was if it was willingly passed on by the hunter it was bonded to; the magic was so powerful in the weapon that it needed to be diffused by its owner before handled by anyone else, and it made the possibility of being bested by one's own blade impossible.

Evelyn spun around on her stool, and I sat in the chair. She cranked me back and swung a light with a magnifying window over the tattoo on my chest. The heat from the light was hot on my skin, and her touch was surprisingly light as she traced over the ink. She leaned down farther, practically lying on top of me, and I could feel the swell of her breast pressed against my stomach. With her head tucked right up under my nose, I took an inadvertent whiff before I could get a handle on myself.

"Don't do that; it's distracting. And creepy."

What was with this chick? I was normally pretty smooth with women, but she had some kind of infernal hate for me.

"Someone really needs to take that tattoo gun away from Sampson. He's not doing anyone any favors over there." She shoved the light out of the way and turned for her equipment. The cold spray of alcohol on my skin startled me and made the muscle underneath jump. "I'm going to shave this spot, so don't move," she warned as she snapped on a pair of rubber gloves and squirted a green soap mixture onto my chest.

Pulling out a disposable razor, she shaved away the chest hair over and around the tattoo. She then smoothed some ointment over the shaved area and turned to dip the end of the gun into one of the ink caps on the counter. Even though she had surgical gloves on, I could still feel the heat of her skin penetrating into mine.

I didn't want to like it, but I did, too much. But, really, what was not to like? She was beautiful. Okay, so there was that little matter of her being a soul-sucking she-shark that hated everything about me, but who didn't like a challenge?

"It looks like Sampson didn't outline correctly, and this spot here," she said, holding the gun and pointing with her pinky, "should extend down another centimeter. There are also accents missing, and I don't think he used the right mixture for the ink either, so I'm going to go over the whole piece again. If the level of the ink mix is off, then the incantation isn't going to work like it should."

She'd also put on a pair of glasses when she'd put on her gloves, plastic black frames with zebra stripes on the inside. She looked up at me through the lenses, and her bright blue eyes looked even bigger than before. "Take a deep breath and let it out; this is going to hurt a bit." With her elbow, she bumped the play button on an iPod plugged into a Zeppelin docking station, and music swirled into the room.

The bite of the needle stung my skin, and I tried not to look at her but couldn't help a peek every now and then. I found myself captivated by the way her eyebrows would furrow together and the way she would chew on the end of her tongue when she concentrated. A piece of her hair that had wiggled its way out of her braid fluttered in her face, and she kept blowing it out of the way. Reaching down, I carefully tucked it behind her ear for her.

She stopped for half a second, and I braced to be read the riot act again.

"Thank you," she said quietly as she started working again and didn't say anything else to me until she was done.

She slathered another layer of ointment over the fresh ink and taped a loose bandage into place. "There's a healing agent in this stuff," she finally said as she smoothed out the last piece of tape. "It's Tessa's own concoction that she puts on me when she does my work. You should be pretty much healed by morning."

"Thanks, you didn't have to do that." I sat up, retrieved my shirt out of the corner, and pulled it over my head.

"Yeah, well, I need you up and running tomorrow so we can get back to your training," she said as she stood and bent backward, cracking her back. She shoved the paper with the phonetic incantation into my hand. "Read it. Let's see if it took this time."

I cleared my throat and read the incantation out loud: "*Veig 'em grest'nth.*" When nothing happened, I was so frustrated I could have spit.

"No, you're saying it wrong," she said, taking the paper from me. "The accent is on the *I* in *veig* and it's a long *E* in *grest'nth*," she explained, marking the emphasis on the sheet. "Try it again and own it. You can't just say the words; you have to feel them. Imagine the magic moving through your body, feel the heat of it in the ink, and embrace it."

I concentrated, thought about everything she'd just said and how she'd said it. With conviction. She might have been a bit of a bitch, but she knew her shit. I also thought about the weight of her body against mine as she had leaned over me, etching into my skin the words I was about to speak.

"Veig 'em grest'nth."

I felt a flicker in my veins, a spark that spread to every extremity, and a burn in my chest where the tattoo lay. When I opened my eyes, I could see a faint glow from the ink even through the bandage under my shirt. "Cool," I marveled.

"Yeah, cool. You can now do something you should have been able to do in week one. Congratulations," she said, rolling her eyes.

Jesus, I'd heard of one step forward and two steps back, but this was ridiculous.

"Look," she continued as we walked out of the shop, "practice the incantation and watch some of the videos from the training ring tonight so you're better prepared in the morning, because I'm not gonna go easy on you tomorrow like I did today."

As Evelyn walked away, I saw a faint glow underneath her hair on the back of her neck. I'd noticed it earlier in her shop whenever she would turn around while she'd been working on me and also in the training ring as she'd left.

At first I thought it was something I set off in her because I'd only seen it when she was irritated with me. But then I remembered the spot hadn't glowed when she'd been in the other room with Zach, and she'd seemed plenty ticked about him pawing at her.

She popped her ear buds in, and I heard her sing the chorus of "Midnight Special" by Creedence Clearwater Revival as she climbed the stairs to the house level.

What kind of mark is on the back of her neck that glowed like that?

I did as Evelyn suggested. I figured she would find something to chew me out for, but this wasn't going to be it. I plugged in my own ear buds and listened to her voice as I watched training video after training video, most of them with her in them. Okay, all of them starred her. She was incredible, and I was utterly transfixed by the way she moved. Her braid whipped around behind her when she spun, determination set in her jaw when she attacked, and the ripple of her thigh muscles under her tight workout pants kept me glued to the screen until I couldn't keep my eyes open anymore. God, there was something seriously hot about a woman who could kick ass.

That night, I lay in my bunk, listening to the sound of her voice on the recording — the way she said the words, when she took a breath, the air of annoyance in the way she sighed before she began speaking. All of it was wonderful and maddening at the same time. The two of us were like oil and water, and we were going to either kill each other or screw each other stupid.

If I had anything to say about it, it would be the latter.

CHAPTER 4
EVELYN

At some ungodly hour the next morning, I was greeted by Tessa grinning down at me.

"Damn it, Tess, it's way too freaking early to be starting with this crap." I rolled over and pulled the covers over my head, trying to get back into the dream I'd been having.

"So I see. Dreaming about someone in particular, hmm?" she asked with a giggle, reaching under the blanket to poke the tattoo on the back of my neck with her boney finger. "I bet I know who," she taunted.

Swatting her hand away, I sat up and glared at that little turd as I hopped out of bed and padded to the bathroom. "For your information, I wasn't dreaming about anyone," I said over my shoulder.

Liar, my inner voice niggled at me.

"Liar," she called, and I could hear the springs of the bed squeak as she got up to follow me. "I mean, really, Ev, why do you even bother trying to sell me a line of bullshit? You know I'm not going to buy it. Besides, your tattoo is glowing like a supernova." Leaning against the doorway of the bathroom, she wore a knowing smirk.

"Geez, T, I'm trying to pee here."

"Fine, at least admit you were dreaming about Daniel and I'll leave you alone." She narrowed her eyes at me.

Damn her.

"Enjoy the show, then," I responded stubbornly as I settled on the seat. She should have known better than anyone she wasn't going to get me to admit anything that easily.

Tess crossed her arms over her chest and glared at me as hard as she could. Never mind the typical "if looks could kill"—"if looks could walk across the room and slap me upside the head" was what I looked in the face. I tried ignoring her as I finished my business, but Tess was kind of hard to ignore. Flushing couldn't even drown her out.

"Evelyn Elizabeth Brighton, I know you know I know," she babbled as I moved to the sink to wash my hands. "I *felt* it in the pit of my stomach how right the two of you are together when I watched you practicing with him yesterday. I saw the way the back of your neck lit up like a Christmas tree when you inspected his 'tattoos,'" she said, pointing an accusing finger in my face.

"What is with all *this* shit?" I mimicked the air-quote action she'd made when she'd said "tattoos."

"This"—she waved her fingers in the air again—"is I'm your best friend, and I know what turns your crank better than anyone, even better than you probably. And I *know* he's turning the hell out of that rusty old crank of yours," she rambled as she followed me into the other room where I changed into my workout clothes.

"Please…him?" I asked, with an overtly dramatic roll of my eyeballs. "Seriously, T, you need to go to the infirmary and get your gut checked out, 'cause I think you're constipated and it's interfering with your mojo."

"Yeah," she snorted. "You just keep telling yourself that the next time he has your ass pinned to the mat in the training ring."

"Whatever," I tossed back over my shoulder as I headed out into the hallway and toward the other end where the guys' room was, determined to not let Tess get under my skin that morning.

Pausing at the closed door with my hand on the knob, I contemplated if I should knock or just barge in. I started to open the door but stopped when I was bombarded with a barrage of *what-ifs*.

What if he was still asleep, all tucked up in his bed? What if he was getting dressed, wandering around in just low-slung sweats and bare feet? What if he was just getting out of the shower, wet and naked?

The last one made me let go of that doorknob like it was on fire. I turned on my heel and headed down the stairs for breakfast. I wasn't his babysitter, I reasoned with myself; he could get his own ass up.

I stopped short on the bottom step when I saw Daniel, looking too hot for his own damn good that early in the morning and sitting in *my* spot at the table eating bacon, eggs, and toast.

"You're in my seat," I said as I picked up a plate and scooped up a spoonful of scrambled eggs.

He turned this way and that in the chair; he even stood up and sat back down again. "I don't see your name on it anywhere," he said, taking a big bite of toast.

"Real mature. Now get your ass out of *my* seat!" I plopped my cup of orange juice on the table so hard some of it sloshed out.

Daniel casually shrugged, grabbed the chair next to him, and slid it underneath his butt, managing to remain in the same position at the table all the while.

"Here," he said with that annoying grin as he pushed the chair he'd been sitting on over to me. I was so going to enjoy kicking his ass that day.

I tossed my plate onto the table with a loud clang, at which point Isolde decided to step in before I stabbed him with my knife and fork.

"All right, you two, save it for the training ring," she warned, sliding a couple of pancakes onto each of our plates. "Evelyn, there are plenty of other places to sit."

Daniel grinned triumphantly, and my blood set to boiling. Why on earth did I let him irritate me so much?

Tessa's voice bounced off the inside of my skull: *"Because he's turning your crank, pushing your buttons, winding you up…take your pick, Evs, because you know they all apply."*

Ugh! I was too frustrated to stay there in the same room with him without punching him in the throat. "Training ring in an hour," I grumbled as I picked up my plate and headed downstairs to eat in my shop.

After finishing my breakfast, I puttered around for the next hour and tried not to think about Daniel. I glared at the chair in the middle of the back room as if he were still perched in it, shirtless with that shit-eating grin plastered across his goddamned face. Once, I almost sat in the chair—after carefully locking the door, of course, so no one would accidentally wander in and find me with my nose pressed to the leather, trying to see if it still smelled like him. And then came the self-inflicted chiding and browbeating for even *thinking* about doing something as ridiculous and lame and downright girlie.

When the hour was almost up, I headed to the training arena, hoping to get a head start on my stretching. Looking through the little round window in the door, I could see Daniel wearing a tank top and knit shorts, swinging his arms and rolling his neck as he warmed up. The muscles in his powerful thighs coiled under his skin as he squatted down and stood back up again. Closing my eyes, I willed out of my head the vision of his lean, toned body glistening with sweat. Things were going to have to change, and fast. Rules. I was going to have to set rules, right there, right then.

"You need to put some pants on, and a shirt, a real shirt, not… that," I ordered as I pushed open the door.

"What? Why?" he asked, looking down at himself.

Why? Because I can't stop thinking about your half-naked sweaty body, that's why.

"Because…" *Quick, Evie, think.* He cocked an eyebrow at me, and I could feel the back of my neck heating up; I whipped my hand up to rub the tattoo. "Look, you're fine for today, but next time wear something more…appropriate."

"I thought I was," he said under his breath.

"Can we just do this already?"

"Fine. After you," he said with a dramatic, sweeping bow and a hefty helping of snark.

As I walked past him, he took me by surprise—wrapping his arm around my neck in a chokehold, he lifted my body off the ground. I could feel his hot breath in my hair and the prickle of his unshaven face on my skin.

"Never turn your back on your opponent," he snarled into my ear.

I sputtered and coughed out a strength spell as I gripped his arm, my feet flailing wildly in the air. The magic coursed through my body like fire, and I jerked his arm away from my throat, heaving his body over my shoulder. He landed with a sound thud on the mat, and the breath whooshed out of his lungs.

"Nice try," I laughed and walked away again.

I could hear him beginning the strength incantation as his foot swept across my legs, knocking them out from under me, and I landed flat on my back. Before I could get my breath, he was on top of me, pinning me to the mat. The top portion of his fresh tattoo was visible through the neck of his shirt. It glowed brightly against his skin, and I could feel the magic vibrating in both of our bodies where they pressed together. I couldn't stop staring at the slice of illuminated ink on his chest or the light sheen of moisture that covered his flesh.

"Pretty cool, huh?" His voice was so soft and smooth, I felt like I could swim in the sound of it.

"Why yes, quite cool, Daniel. How's that crank, Ev? Is it turnin'? I'm guessin' yeah," a little annoying voice chirped from the doorway.

I jerked my head back in an attempt to shoot laser beams out of my eyes at Tessa and somehow managed to whack Daniel on the chin, knocking his teeth together.

I swear, I may actually have to kill her.

"What do you want, Tess?" I asked, rubbing the top of my head where it had connected with his jaw.

"Yeah, um, Alex wants to see you, ya know, whenever you can manage to shimmy out from under Daniel." She giggled. "Take your time," she sang as she backed out of the training room.

She was so dead.

Daniel let me up, and I instructed him on some moves to practice on the bag before I trotted down the hall to Alexander's office.

"You wanted to see me?"

"Yes, I have an assignment for you," he said excitedly.

"In addition to the pain in the ass you've already assigned me to?" I hooked my thumb over my shoulder. He raised a disapproving eyebrow in my direction. "Sorry," I said, albeit begrudgingly.

"Very good." He gave a weird little smile, and I got a sneaking suspicion that he'd been talking to Tess lately. Damn her, I was going to staple her lips shut one of those days.

"I hope his training is going well, because he'll be joining you on your assignment this afternoon."

"Are you kidding me? He's not ready," I protested. "He just learned how to use his strength; he's cocky, belligerent, insubordinate; he's going to get somebody killed, and…" The entire time I ranted, Alex continued to smile and nod in agreement. "And let me guess, these are the same things you used to say about me, right?"

"Used to? I said something to that effect to corporate two days ago when I was told to assign Daniel to you. Tessa already has your paperwork and is walking Daniel's handler, Christopher, through the preparation process. It's just a test run to see how he handles himself with otherworlders."

"Fine, but don't blame me if he winds up dead." I slunk out into the hallway.

"If who winds up dead?" Daniel asked, sauntering down the hall with a towel slung across the back of his neck.

"You, genius," I said as I passed him. "We're going out. You and I have an assignment this afternoon."

As we walked into the shop, Tessa had Chris fetching ingredients for evoking a masking spell, standard procedure on a mission of any kind. Hell, as hunters we needed it just to go out in public after we'd been branded. Creatures of the underworld had a sixth sense for us after we'd been marked.

Daniel watched in wonder as Tess measured out two piles of an iridescent blue powder, one for me and one for him.

"Where we going, T?" I took a seat on one of the counters along the back wall.

"Vladimir," she said, adding a heaping scoop of the blue bonding agent onto a scale to weigh it. She looked up at me, and I could see the worry on her face. She was going heavy on this mix; she must have had one of her bad feelings about this assignment.

"Who's Vladimir?" Daniel asked.

"A Romanian goblin that runs a little apothecary shop outside of Chinatown," Tess explained. "He carries the majority of our in-cantation stock ingredients in the highest grade, and he stocks it on site." She poured the powder combinations into two envelopes and set them aside.

"Wait, so our assignment is to basically go grocery shopping?" Daniel asked with a laugh.

"This isn't a joke, Daniel," I chided as I hopped off the counter to pull two candles out of the drawer. "Everything we do outside of these walls has to be taken very seriously, no matter how menial and beneath you it may seem."

"I'm sorry, I didn't think—"

"Exactly, you didn't think, and that's what's going to get us both killed. Have you ever even worked a cloaking spell before?" I reached for a casting pot.

"I've heard of it, but I've never performed it myself." His face changed, as if he was finally taking in the seriousness of what I said, and, for some reason, I felt bad for yelling at him.

"Look, I'm not trying to bust your balls or be a bitch. I can only assume that Alex knows your level of inexperience and saw this as an opportunity for you to learn how to mask your presence to others in the outside world. You walk out there unprepared and you might as well walk into a lion's den wearing a pork chop necklace because everything and its brother will have sniffed out, drawn, and quartered you before you even know what's hit you. This isn't the middle of the Nevada desert where the nearest otherworlders are a hundred miles away; you're in the big leagues now, and they practically live next door."

"Yeah, I get it." He nodded, his lip twitching as he gripped the ends of the towels still hanging around his neck. I was pretty sure he was irritated with me, but he'd just have to get over it.

"Good, then be back here in an hour."

I thought about a lot of things while I went through my shower ritual, a lot of things I normally thought about when I prepared for an assignment. But mostly, I thought about Tess adding the extra binding agent to the incantation mix and how her eyes, worried and protective, kept cutting to Daniel. Was he in danger?

Stepping out of the bathroom, I saw a folded note on my pillow next to a lead-crystal dagger encased in a leather holster:

Watch him closely and keep this handy, just in case. ~T

This dagger wasn't something we used often; it was heavy and awkward, but it was the most effective on thick goblin skin.

I dressed and strapped the dagger to my side, hidden just under my coat but easily accessible. After whipping my damp hair into a quick braid, I headed down the stairs. I had to talk to Alex; the urge to protect Daniel was almost overpowering, and hopefully I could convince him that the best place for Daniel was there where it was safe. Everyone knew he wasn't ready for this.

As I rounded the corner, I saw Daniel with his nose buried in an old book full of incantations outside of the shop and right in my path to Alexander's office. He was early, which told me he was eager to go out. So much for sneaking by and having a chat with Alex. This was going to happen whether I wanted it to or not.

Daniel's lips moved slightly with the words as he read, and for a split second I wondered what they would feel like on mine. They looked so warm and full, as if they were made for kissing. I shook my head and cursed myself for allowing that indulgent thought. What the hell was happening to me? That clown had been there for a day, and I was already thinking about kissing him? This was all Tess's fault for putting that damned idea of Daniel in my head that morning. I needed to focus, concentrate, if I was to be expected to not only look after my own ass, but his as well.

"Let's go," I said as I brushed past him and into the shop. He smelled crisp and clean, and I inwardly cringed at the thought of anything happening to him. I would never forgive myself.

Everything we needed for our spell was set up in back. Two stone casting pots, two maroon candles, and two envelopes sat on the counter. I closed the door and tried not to think about Tessa's warning too much while Daniel and I stood side by side in the small yellow room. But the bulging belly of the envelopes made it hard.

"Pour this into the pot carefully," I said as I handed him one of the packets and slid one of the casting pots over to him. I was surprised when he listened and watched studiously as I emptied the contents into my pot before he did the same. "Do you have fire? A lighter or some matches?" I asked, passing him one of the candles.

"No, should I?"

In any other situation, I would have read him the riot act for not knowing something so basic, but now wasn't the time. He needed his confidence and wits about him. Digging into my front pocket, I pulled out a disposable lighter.

"Always have fire," I said as I tossed him the Bic and reached down and popped a chrome lighter out of my Lucky 13 Deathfly belt buckle, "and always have a spare."

I made him recite the one-word incantation out of the book that was propped up behind the casting pots. I had to correct his pronunciation and cadence three times, but he finally got it. We lit our candles, repeated the ancient word five times, and touched our candles to the powder.

There was a quick flash of purple smoke, and a shockwave of magic rolled through the room, dissipating like heat curling off the pavement in the summertime. Daniel struggled to wipe an amazed grin off his face when he saw me looking at him, replacing it with a sterner, more serious expression.

"It's okay. That part is pretty cool," I admitted with a reassuring smile as we headed out to the garage.

Under my name on a pegboard dangled a set of keys to this assignment's vehicle. Josie and Meg were meticulous about their stock and had a penchant for vintage classics.

"1969 Chevrolet El Camino," Daniel whispered as we walked up to the side of the car. "Can I drive?"

"Hell no," Josie hollered from across the garage. "Strictly shotgun, rookie." She grinned and strolled up behind Daniel to give him the official Josephine Mira once-over. "I'm Josie, and these are my babies" — she gestured to the myriad of cars — "and you, hon', you are very pretty."

"Leave him alone, Josie," I said. "You're gonna make him lose focus, and we have to get going before he loses his magic." I pulled the driver's side door open and slid in.

"Fine. Go get 'em, tiger," she drawled, reaching back and giving him a hearty swat on the backside as she walked away, her hand lingering a second or two longer than it should have.

"Is she always like that?" Daniel asked as he sank into the passenger's seat.

"Pretty much," I chuckled and turned the key to rev up the engine. The intro to Guns N' Roses's "Paradise City" echoed out of the speakers — Meg went all the way when she hooked you up with wheels, and that included apropos tunes. "Just try to relax. Focus on the music; it helps."

He nodded and sucked in a deep breath and blew it out as we rolled out of the garage. We wound down Mulholland and through Studio City until we hit Cahuenga Boulevard to the 101 South and into downtown Los Angeles.

Daniel didn't say anything for the entire twenty-five-minute drive. He bobbed his head to the music as though actually listening to it, but I could practically see the wheels turning in his mind. If I had to guess, I'd have bet he was going over the plan in his head. His lips pursed as he stared out the window, the scruff on his face rippling as he clenched his jaw. I knew where he was going in his head too, that silent and deadly place hunters go before an assignment, and damn if it wasn't sexy as hell on him in particular. When I parked in back of Vlad's shop, I noticed Daniel take another long, slow breath.

"He's going to try to get inside your head. Keep your concentration and you'll be fine," I said as I reached over and gave him a reassuring pat on the leg.

"I know," he snapped. "I've done my research. I'm not idiot enough to go into someplace completely blind."

God, I'd never wanted to slug someone just as much as I wanted to kiss him as I did with this guy.

Pulling open the door, an electronic-sensor ping announced our entry as we walked into what appeared to be an old-fashioned apothecary. Bottles, vials, and decanters of every size lined the walls, along with a long oak table in the middle of the room that housed a variety of scales for measuring any multitude of items.

"'Ello, greetings, and hi! What is it that I can help you buy?" Vladimir called as he moved the curtain leading to the back area and appeared across the room. His brown, leathery goblin mouth twisted into a wide toothy smile. "Evie, I thought I smelled you. It is good to see you, this is true." He rushed across the shop with his arms open as if greeting an old friend.

"What's my rule, V?" I asked, my hand itching to reach for the crystal dagger tucked against my side. I hated that goblins only spoke in rhyme; it was creepy.

Vladimir stopped where he was and took one step backward. "Yes, yes, I must be always three steps away from thee." He sniffed the air. He looked like some kind of demonic dog until his grin stretched to an unnatural width, his black eyes zeroing in on Daniel. "And what have we here that I smell? You are new, I can tell." His gnarled hands twisted in front of his diminutive body as he continued to take copious whiffs of the surrounding air. "What of you, hunter new? Do you require three steps too?" he asked, a little too excitedly for my liking.

"No," I said, not even giving Daniel a chance to answer for himself. "Tessa's rule with this one, got it?"

"What's Tessa rule?" Daniel asked as I pulled the list of supplies out of my back pocket.

"Three times three, it will be, the distance between you and me," Vladimir answered, taking six steps backward.

As I moved about the shop, gathering the items from my list, I noticed that Vlad's eyes never strayed from Daniel. He watched him like a hawk and licked his lips way too much for my liking. Vlad was on the wagon, sworn off the consumption of human organs and flesh, but I was getting a bad feeling about his strength holding out where fresh hunter meat was concerned. And who could blame him? I'd been wanting to take a bite out of Daniel for the last hour.

Daniel must have sensed the eyes on him too because he hovered around the front of the store near the door, looking at everything. But he wasn't just browsing; he was taking inventory of his surroundings and moving along the outskirts of the shop, never leaving his back vulnerable. That was the sign of a good hunter.

I placed vials of liquid and decanters of powder into a wooden box and took note that Vlad had managed to weasel his way a step closer to Daniel. I almost said something to him—heck, I almost flew across the room and gutted that wormy little goblin—but one look from Danny reassured me that he had the situation handled.

I continued gathering my items as Vladimir took another bold step toward the door and Daniel.

"Yes, I am fine with the liver that is porcine or bovine," he said, swiping the back of his hand across his mouth to mop up an errant string of drool. "But if the choice were mine and I could find a glass of vintage goblin wine, I would surely dine at a half-past nine on the liver that is thine."

"Vladimir, knock it off. We don't want to have to kill you today," I warned, but my words seemed to fall on deaf ears as he continued to speak and move closer to Daniel.

"It would be quite easy to extract, three quick strikes to be exact."

The air crackled with the sensation of Daniel's magic ramping up. He was letting his anger get the better of him. Crap, he didn't have the training to pull two spells at once; if he tried invoking his strength, he would lose the spell covering his scent and then we would both be screwed.

"Thrice the slice and it will be a fine supper for little me," Vlad hissed.

Watching the scene unfold on the opposite side of the store, I realized I would not be able to make it over there in time to stop Vladimir.

Shit. I dropped the box with a loud clang and reached for the crystal dagger in my jacket.

"Hunter new, so clean and fresh, how I'll feast upon your flesh!" the goblin shouted, and he sailed through the air.

Moving faster than I'd ever seen him move, Daniel hooked his arm around the back of Vladimir's head in a blur and cranked his unholy body backward, snapping the creature's neck. But, unfortunately, while that move had emitted a truly gruesome sound, it did nothing to stop the beast—his green teeth gnashing and snarling—from trying to rip off a piece of Daniel's flesh.

"Daniel!" I called as I ran toward him and hurtled the dagger across the expanse of the store.

Catching the ancient weapon with his free hand, he sank it into Vladimir's exposed chest, piercing the goblin's heart.

"Get down!" he shouted as he jerked the blade free of the dead body.

I didn't ask any questions; I acted on our combined instinct. Still in the midst of an all-out run, I dropped to my knees and leaned back, sliding under the long oak table in the middle of the store.

As I cleared the underside of the table, I could see Daniel running toward me—it looked like he was moving in slow motion as he leapt over my head. I heard the loud clunk of his boot planting in the center of the table before I saw him vault himself at the female goblin that had been sneaking up behind me.

He maneuvered with a precision and skill beyond his training. His instincts were spot-on. It was an incredible sight, and if I hadn't seen it with my own eyes, I never would have believed it. He was beauty personified. He was also pulling heavy on his strength spell, which left his presence exposed to any otherworlders that might have been nearby.

I had to move fast. Scrambling over the table, I practically tackled him to the ground, chanting the transfer incantation and pushing as much of my magic toward him as I could.

"Um, you're welcome," he said as I felt his arms wrap around my back.

"Shhh, concentrate on your concealing spell before we have the entire Mogwai district in here trying to eat us for lunch," I scolded. We were on the borders of Chinatown, home to one of the wickedest demon clans in the Los Angeles area.

Once Daniel got his magic stabilized, I wriggled out of his arms and reached a hand down to help him up. "For the record, I could have handled that by myself, but thanks for having my back."

"No problem, I knew there was a female lurking around and that as soon as I killed her mate, she'd try to go after mine," he said, handing me the crystal dagger.

"I'm not your mate." It probably came out a lot harsher than I'd meant it to, but only because the thought freaked me out more than I wanted to admit, even to myself.

"I know that, but she didn't," he shot back, clearly offended.

Trying to get off the whole mate subject, I asked, "How did you know there was another?"

"There were two cups." He pointed to the bistro table in the corner.

"So? He could have had a friend over for tea earlier."

"One is bigger than the other. Male goblins always dote on their mates, so he would have provided her with a larger portion," he explained.

Impressive; someone had been doing his homework. Smart was definitely sexy on him.

After calling for a cleanup crew, we started putting the list items back into the wooden box that had been knocked over in the scuffle.

"Hey, Evelyn," Daniel said as he dropped in another bundle of candles, "um…thanks."

"For what?"

"Having my back."

"Yeah, well, the last thing I need is to have a rookie die on my watch."

I picked up the wooden box and headed out the back door to the car.

CHAPTER 5
DANIEL

Evie and I trained relentlessly in the days after our outing, and I'd be the first to admit that I thoroughly enjoyed every minute of it—from getting up at the butt crack of dawn to beat her downstairs to the kitchen to pinning each other to the mat in the ring. I did love getting a rise out of her…it was better than no reaction at all.

One morning I found a piece of duct tape on the back of the chair with "Evie" scribbled on it in her sloppy handwriting. So, I did the only thing I could do: I pulled the tape off and slapped it onto the neighboring chair. Of course, that pissed her off, and I ended up with a black eye and bloody nose in practice that day.

The next day, I came down and Evelyn was already sitting in the coveted spot, glaring at the staircase and clutching a fork-like weapon, waiting for me. I opted to swipe a bagel and two banana nut muffins off the counter and a couple of juice boxes out of the fridge, then headed for the weapons room instead of waiting for Isolde to fix a full meal and risk getting a fork to the neck.

"What, no fancy sit-down breakfast this morning?" Chris asked as I tossed a muffin and a juice box onto the table in front of him.

"Nope, my keen hunter senses told me that this was not a good morning to poke the barracuda."

"Ya know, a good poke might be just what the old barracuda needs." He grinned, waggling his eyebrows while he chewed a piece of his muffin.

I took a chunk of my bagel and threw it at him. "Shut up, asshole."

"Oh, come on. You'd jump on her like a lion on a gazelle and you know it."

"It's a moot point, my friend. She hates me with the burning white-hot passion of a thousand suns."

"She does not," Chris scoffed, picking up a pastry and shoving it in his mouth. "Quit being such a pussy. You know as well as I do that mad sex is hot sex." He had me there. "What about that spell we were working on? That had to make some kind of impression on her, right?"

I thought back to the day before. I'd been studying my ass off whenever I wasn't in the ring with Evelyn. Her handler, Tessa, had given Chris some of the incantation books, complete with annotations, for me to read. Some of the notes marked what spells worked well for what, and some were a phonetic spelling of the harder words. Looked like I wasn't the only one who'd had a hard time with these basically extinct languages. After combing through them, we had found a simple spell I could work. I'd practiced hard, and it had been working…against Chris, anyway.

When the time came to use it against Evelyn, she'd been really giving it to me in the ring for what I'd pulled at breakfast. She was like a machine, and I'd been on my back more than I'd been on my feet. Not that I'm complaining; being under her wasn't exactly unpleasant. However, by the time I'd gotten my nose to finally stop bleeding for the third time that day, I'd felt the flesh around my left eye start to swell shut and had had about enough of her big-bad-bitch shit:

"Got one more round in ya, noob?" Evelyn asked as she circled me like a lioness.

God, I hated it when she called me that. I tossed my towel to the floor and got into position, nodding. "Yeah, I got one more in me."

Her lip twitched up in a devious little grin. I'd noticed that she always did that before knocking me on my ass, but this time I was going to be ready.

I could see her mouth barely moving; she was cooking magic, and the strength incantation tattoo over her right breast glowed under her shirt.

Not that I was intentionally staring at her chest—that just happened to be where the tattoo was. Looking at her rack was just a perk.

I grinned and steadied myself as I whispered the spell Chris and I had worked on, a blocking invocation so she would bounce off me like a quarter.

Evie ran at me full bore, and her body connected with mine with a loud smack. I sailed backward through the air like a rag doll, arms and legs flailing, the very breath pounded out of my lungs as I landed with a resounding thud and skidded across the mat a good foot. Even the windows of the training room rattled with the force she'd used.

It took a good couple of seconds before I could get a breath, and by that time, Evelyn was standing over me. "The next time you try to pull magic against me like that, I'll break your arm, got it?"

"Yeah," I choked out, struggling to stand up, but she shoved me back down with her foot.

"Always defend yourself, even if you think you have the upper hand. Being overconfident and arrogant will only get you killed, understand?"

"Got it. Jesus," I said, shoving at her foot.

"Your accents were perfect; I'll give you that much. But you were staring at my boobs, and that broke your concentration," she said, and she headed toward the door and exited the practice ring without so much as another word or glance in my direction.

"Yeah, man," I said to Chris, pointing to my eye, "not so much with the impressing." Luckily, Tess and Isolde were amazing with their healing mojo. As a matter of fact, my eye was barely swollen anymore. My ego, on the other hand, was taking a serious beating, and I was done being treated like a second-rate hunter.

"Well, hello, what have we in here?" an accented, feminine voice asked.

I turned in my chair and saw a tall blonde standing in the doorway. If was honest, she was hot and had that whole Eastern European thing going. But she was no Evelyn, not by a long shot.

"Lana, lead hunter out of the Northern Canadian branch," she said, extending her hand out to me.

"Dan Summers," I said, taking her hand and giving it a good shake. "This is my handler, Chris. We were just transferred here from Nevada for training."

"Interesting, I didn't know Alex was still training new recruits," she mused, sounding very much like Natasha from the old *Bullwinkle* cartoons.

"Oh, he's not. Evelyn is heading up Dan's training," Chris piped up.

"Really," she said with a grin. "Well, that is interesting indeed. And where is dear Evelyn this morning?"

Probably upstairs, cursing me to hell and back for something like, I don't know…breathing.

"Having breakfast, I believe. I just wanted to get some study time in before we hit the practice ring," I said, picking up the first book my hand landed on and holding it up.

A big tattooed hand slid around Lana's slim waist as Zach stepped up behind her. "My room's empty, baby. How about we pick up where we left off the last time you were here," he said before acknowledging either Chris or me. "Oh, hey, guys," he added with a grin.

"Of course, my darling, but first I would like to see what our new little friend here has learned in his training," she cooed as she stretched up onto her toes and kissed his now pouting bottom lip.

"Yeah, ya know, I'm gonna have to pass. Evie is sort of particular about that kind of thing." Case in point: my still slightly swollen eyeball.

"Oh, come on. Prove to me that the mighty Evelyn Brighton has what it takes to train the likes of you. You are just brimming with potential. Your skin practically vibrates with it."

She was goading me and I knew it. There was obviously some animosity between Evie and this chick, but, God help me, I had an almost uncontrollable urge to defend Evelyn's honor.

"All right, you're on. Let's go."

Chris caught my arm on the way out. "As your handler, I should advise against this, but as your friend, I say kick her ass."

I gave him a pat on the back and headed down the corridor to the practice ring. I had to do this. Something inside me had to prove to Lana that Evie was a good trainer. I also wanted to prove to myself that I was worthy of her training, that I wasn't wasting her time as she'd have liked me to believe most of the time — that I had worth, damn it.

The door leading into the ring swung closed, and as soon as I turned around, I saw Lana flying at me, no warning whatsoever. She tackled me to the ground, straddling my waist.

"That was too easy. Perhaps you should train with me; I can teach you so many things," she purred, running her hands up over my chest as she leaned down and sucked my earlobe into her mouth with a wet slurp.

Ew.

Granted, it had been a long time since little Danny had seen any action — and, to a degree, the attention was nice — but still, *ew.* That wasn't what I wanted. Not like that and most definitely not with her. I gathered my strength and shoved her off me as I rolled away, vaulting to my feet.

"No thanks. I'm good."

"Oh, I'm sure you are," she said, the words rolling off her tongue like a proposition. A sultry smile spread across her face, and her eyes sparked with a wicked fire. She came at me again, but this time I was ready, or so I thought. I breathed the strength spell and ducked her advance. I spun on her quickly and brought her to the mat, pinning her for the victory of that move. But before I could get up and ready myself for the next round, she locked her legs around my waist.

"Why you so fast to run away? Maybe I can help you in other areas, hmm?" Her hand slid down and gripped my buttock, hard, and my body, being male and having a mind of its own, reacted to a pretty woman's touch.

"Look, Lan—" was all I got out before she flipped me onto my back and sat on top of me like she had before. "Lana—" I tried to say again, but this time she leaned over and pressed a finger to my lips.

"Shush, you talk too much," she purred, and the next thing I knew, her tongue was halfway down my throat.

I wish I could say that it was moderately pleasant, but damn it, I couldn't breathe. That chick must have been part snake, because I think she licked my tonsils at one point. Not to mention, she tasted like the remnants of the previous night's garlic-laden dinner and cigarettes.

"You wanna get your ass off of my student, Ivan?" I heard as the door closed with a loud slam.

Lana extracted herself from my mouth with a loud, overtly dramatic smacking sound and glared across the room. "I am not Russian. I am from Ukraine," she grumbled.

"Don't really give a shit," Evie said with a shrug. "Now, remove yourself before I remove you."

"I'd like to see you try," Lana said.

Evelyn clearly seethed at the challenge, and her power rolled across the room like a wave. It was everywhere: the paint on the walls, the wood floor under the foam mat, hanging in the air, even in me. It touched everything in the room — except Lana. She had so much control it was astounding.

I saw the flicker of her tongue behind her teeth as Evie whipped out a series of spells. There was a glow beneath the fabric of Evie's workout pants, banded around the top of each thigh, and, without warning, she launched herself so far and so fast I could hardly believe it. I'd never seen another human being move like she did in that moment. She flew over my body, scooping up Lana and pinning her to the opposite wall by the throat, a good two inches off the floor.

"Evelyn, that's enough. I think you've made your point," Alexander said, standing in the open doorway with the rest of the crew behind him, completely agog at what they saw.

The sound of Lana's sputters for air echoed in the room as Evelyn slowly uncurled her fingers, one by one, dropping the taller woman to the floor. Lana staggered across the room and toward the door.

"My apologies," Lana choked out as she passed Alexander.

"Noted," he nodded, never taking his eyes off Evelyn until he turned to escort our guest off the property.

As I sat up, I looked across the room at Evie, sitting on a bench against the back wall. Her knee bounced up and down as she weaved her fingers together and twisted them around.

"Listen," she finally said, "I don't care who you screw or whatever, just not on my time and not in my house, okay?"

"What?" I asked, completely dumbfounded. Did she honestly think I was a willing participant in that? Of course she did; she'd walked in on a Ukrainian Sleestak giving my larynx a tongue bath. "Wait—" I started to explain as I got up off the floor, but she put up her hand.

"Just get your shit together and meet me in the shop," she said quickly and rushed out of the room.

Swiping the two towels off the floor, I tossed them into the hamper just outside the door and hurried after Evelyn. Watching her go ape-shit on Lana had every molecule in my body singing with desire. Damn, I'd thought she was sexy when she was pissed at *me*, but this? It was all I could do not to grab her the second we were alone. I wanted—no, I *needed* her to know what had really happened. I shouldn't have cared what she thought, but I did, damn it.

By the time I made it into Evie's shop, she was already in the back room. She was quiet, quieter than she'd ever been before, which was weird. She usually yelled for me to get my ass in there before I could even get through the door.

"Got a minute?" I asked.

"Yeah," she said without turning around. She never turned around to talk to me, especially in there. "Listen, you lose focus in the ring, in close combat, and I know what can help you with that."

"Evie—"

"Jesus, will you just sit down in the chair and shut up for once? God, you're so…so…you're a guy, Daniel. Rubbing one out in the shower isn't always enough to ease the tension; I get it. Lana is tall, blond, drop-dead gorgeous, and willing, and you're stuck with me, barking orders and snapping at you like a barracuda. Now take off your shirt."

Shit, she knew I called her a barracuda?

I pulled my shirt over my head and saw the tension in her shoulders as she gripped the counter in front of her. There was the familiar glow on the back of her neck again, peeking out from underneath her braid. According to Tess, if I wanted to know what that was, I was going to have to ask Evelyn about it, and she wasn't exactly forthcoming when it came to personal information.

Moving right in behind her, I let my fingers skim across the top of her shoulder as I gently pushed her braid aside. Under the thick plait of hair was a multitude of delicate swirls and intricate shapes surrounding an eye tattooed onto her creamy skin. Pinks, purples, and soft blues made up the ink palette.

"What is this, anyway?" I asked, tracing my index finger over the design. It glowed brighter, and I could feel her flesh quiver under my touch.

"It's nothing," she said quietly, but she didn't try to make me stop yet. "It has nothing to do with being a hunter, it's…personal."

"I like it," I said, leaning down for a closer look. "It's pretty, suits you." My lips were so close to her skin that it was all I could do to keep from kissing the back of her neck like I wanted to. "Why does it glow like that?"

The hint of a smile that had been on her face melted back into her usual, stern Evelyn demeanor, and her body stiffened as she abruptly swatted my hand away. "Because you irritate the piss out of me. Now sit down." She moved as far away from me as she could in the closed space of the room.

I had gotten so many mixed signals from her and felt there was more to this whole glowing business than she'd let on. I'd have to look into it myself if I wanted to know any more, but at least I knew something about it: it was personal. That wasn't an incantation she had put on for battle; it was something she'd wanted there. It had meaning, and come Hell or high water I was going to find out what it was.

As I sat back in the big chair, she moved her tools to a stainless steel tray, draped a blue sterile towel on my left side, and rolled her stool over. She wore a headband to hold her hair back this time and donned those damned glasses again that fed some weird sexy-librarian fantasy I had as she prepared the skin left-of-center on my chest. I ran the gamut of unpleasant thoughts to distract myself from the fact that her palm was laying square on my nipple.

"Can you reach the play button?" she asked, nodding toward her iPod plugged into the docking station. I stretched over and pushed play, and an acoustic version of "Personal Jesus" started. "Deep breath," she warned before she touched the needle to my flesh.

The buzz was so soothing and I was so relaxed that I chanced a look down at her. I couldn't help it—she was undeniably amazing to watch, no matter what she was doing.

"What does this one mean?" I asked looking at the outline of five interlocking circles.

"You ask a lot of questions, do you know that?"

"Well, how am I supposed to learn anything if I don't ask?"

She stopped tattooing, looked up at me, and shoved her glasses up her nose with her knuckle. I think she was genuinely shocked that I hadn't just zipped it like I usually did. Or she was pissed, again.

"It's a Celtic five-fold," she said as she leaned down and started working where she'd left off. "The four outer rings symbolize several different things, depending on the lore you read."

"Such as?"

"Such as the four elements, the seasons. Some say their meaning is based in ruling, tenet, or even ritualistic beliefs. The fifth ring, of course, is what binds them all and gives balance," she explained while she worked.

"Well, what do you believe?"

"All of them and none of them at the same time, I guess." She wiped off the excess ink.

"How do you manage that one?" I chuckled.

"Don't move." She shot a quick glare as my chest moved up and down with my laugh. When I promised to stay still, she turned to replenish her ink supply and continued. "I believe that it means something different to everyone and that it means what you need it to mean, when you need it to mean it. I know that probably makes no sense, but it's what works for me."

"No, actually, it makes perfect sense."

Evelyn looked up at me for a moment, over the black plastic frames of her glasses and through her eyelashes, before she started to work again. I continued to watch her while the needle pricked at my skin, and the buzzing of the gun soothed the knot twisting away in my gut.

Unfortunately, the piece was small, and in no time at all she was cleaning up. She rolled across the room on her stool and pulled an old glass decanter out of the cupboard. *Tess's Special Brew* was written on a label stuck to the side; I hadn't noticed that before. I recognized the handwriting immediately from the duct tape on the back of the chair in the kitchen the day before. It made me smile that she would take the time to label the jar, given no one else would see it but her and Tessa.

"Rest and study for the remainder of the day. Go take care of some guy business if you have to—I'm sure Lana hasn't gone too far yet—but make sure to cloak up before you go. Tess can hook you up with what you need, just be back for training at the usual time tomorrow," she said as she cleaned up the unused ink and disposable parts and readied the rest for sterilization.

"Thanks, I appreciate that," I said, carefully pulling on my shirt.

She only nodded in response, her jaw clenched and her fists squeezed so tightly that her knuckles were white. I probably should have let her believe that Lana was what I wanted and let her stew about that all night for all the crap she'd been giving me since I'd been there. But I couldn't; two wrongs didn't make a right.

"She was the one who challenged me, ya know. I tried to tell her that it wasn't a good idea, that you wouldn't approve of it, and that's when she started in," I explained without letting her interrupt. "She didn't think you had what it took to train me and offered to take over, so I wanted to prove her wrong. But she pinned me and basically propositioned me right there on the training room floor."

Evelyn scoffed and shook her head in disbelief, but I continued.

"I told her I wasn't interested, but she grabbed my ass and shoved her tongue down my throat. That's when you came in."

"Thanks," she said with sort of a half smile that I could tell she was trying like hell to hide. I was making progress; she didn't seem to hate everything about me, at least not right then.

"And for the record," I said, "anything that I need or want is in this house." *In this very room,* but I wasn't about to tell her that.

I turned and headed out of the shop.

CHAPTER 6
EVELYN

I felt the weight of Daniel's finger on the back of my neck, tracing the lines of my tattoo, for the remainder of the day. Even curled up in my bed at night, I could still feel the heat from his bare chest on my back and the warm caress of his breath against my skin. His voice was like a whisper in my ear, and it made the little hairs on the back of my neck stand on end. I should have stopped him from getting that close, but once he'd touched me, it was all I could have done to keep my composure.

Hell, I hated to admit that I would have been content to let him stroke the back of my neck all the livelong day if he hadn't brought up the glowing. But, naturally, Daniel didn't know when to shut up, a trait of his that tested me time and again, whether it was combating in the ring or lying back in my tattoo chair. The latter of which I liked far too much for my own good.

That last week I'd been hard on him, I admitted. But I knew that I needed to be. Something big was coming; I could feel it. We all could—even Daniel felt it for all of his inexperience. It was part of our DNA as hunters.

Rounding the corner into the weapons room the next day, intent on dragging Daniel back into the ring to resume his training, I saw him sitting at a table with Tony and Z. In front of each one of them was a fully assembled MK16, a weapon that I felt was more Tony and Z's style than Daniel's—he was too good, too precise in what I'd seen him do so far to need such a heavy weapon. A good hunter didn't need anything like that to get the job done; all I needed was my blade, a .45, and a good hearty spell. Anything else was just for show, in my opinion.

Poised on the other side of the table were their respective handlers, Chris, Walter, and Finn, each clutching a stopwatch.

Daniel looked up, and I could see the defeated expression on his face.

"Sorry, guys, we'll have to do this another time. I have to get back to training," he said. He pushed his chair back and stood up.

"Bullshit, man," Tony said, shoving him back into his chair as he glanced over at me and gave me the stink-eye. "C'mon, Evs, don't be such a hard-ass. One round, that's it. You can even count us off. I know how you like to be in charge and all."

"Yeah, she does," Z said with a wink and a skeevy grin.

"Ugh," I groaned and rolled my eyes at Z's lewd comment.

"It's a minute and a half out of your day, at the most," Tony pled.

Six sets of puppy-dog eyes stared over at me, but the ones that got to me were Daniel's big blue ones and those pouty lips of his. *Damn it.*

"Fine," I relented, biting the inside of my lip so I wouldn't smile at the spark that lit up Daniel's face. "One, two—"

"Wait, wait, wait! I'm not ready!" Tony hollered, proceeding to make a big show of cracking his knuckles, shaking his hands out, and emitting a myriad of strange noises in preparation. "Okay, now I'm ready."

"Anyone else?" I asked.

"Nope, I'm good," Z replied, lounging back in his seat. This was a game he and Tony played on occasion. Z *always* won, and it drove Tony absolutely nuts.

"Ready," Daniel said, never looking up. He sat on the other side of Tony and stared down at his rifle, his hands lying relaxed in his lap.

"On your mark…"

Z picked an invisible piece of lint off his shirt, Tony snapped straight in his chair, and Daniel looked very much at peace, still staring at his weapon.

"Get set…"

Z yawned and straightened in his chair, Tony gripped the table so hard I thought a chunk was going to break off, and Daniel remained very calm and almost Zen-like.

"Go!"

The clang of metal rifle pieces hitting the wooden table reverberated off the walls of the small room as they began to dismantle their weapons.

Tony looked like he was about to come apart at the seams; his eyes darted back and forth, checking the progress of his two opponents. One thing about Tony: he hated to lose. He would cheat if he thought he could get away with it for even half a second.

As usual, Z worked at a steady pace, which was about two seconds ahead of Tony. And, as usual, he knew he had him beat, so the complacent dip-shit cackled just to mess with Tony's head. But what Z couldn't see was Daniel, working on the other side of Tony and a good three seconds ahead of Z.

Daniel peeked up once and suppressed a grin when he caught me staring at him. Blatantly. But in my defense, Finn and Walter were staring pretty damn hard themselves. It couldn't be helped. He had taken that thing apart and put it back together like he'd come out of the womb with one in his hands.

"Done," Daniel proclaimed, laying his fully assembled rifle on the table in front of him.

"Forty-nine-point-eight seconds," Chris announced with a proud grin.

"Very impressive, Daniel," Alexander said as he lightly applauded from the doorway. It was really scary how Alex could sneak into a room full of hunters without a soul hearing him. I aspired to that. "Would you, Evelyn, and Christopher, accompany me to the conference room, please?"

Ugh, here we go again. More shit I'm not gonna like doing.

"Good afternoon," Alex said as I took my seat between Daniel and Tess, who was already in the room. "A last-minute assignment has come through, and it is one that must be handled immediately: a small nest of Limaske demons. Evelyn, you and Daniel have been chosen to carry out this assignment before nightfall."

Limaske were a breed of demon that usually converged in small packs of no more than three or four. They were very hard to dispose of due to the fact that they had a beyond superb sense of hearing. I had the utmost respect for Alex and his decisions, but what he was suggesting was virtually impossible. If I had a fully trained, experienced hunter to partner with, we could do it. As a matter of fact, solo would be ideal and totally doable. But having to drag Daniel along for the ride was only going to get us both killed. I opened my mouth to protest, but Alex stopped me before I could even verbalize my concerns.

"Tessa and Christopher have found a spell that will link your minds for the duration of the assignment," he said with a nod to the pair of handlers.

"What does that mean, exactly?" Daniel asked skeptically, shooting Chris the hairy-eyeball. It appeared his handler hadn't shared that little nugget of info with him either.

"It's perfectly safe," Tess said defensively. I tended to worry when she opened with that remark. "Chris and I tested it, and it works… great." She stifled a giggle, and I could have sworn I saw the two of them blush. Why did I get the distinct feeling I was not going to like where this was going?

"After Tess performs the spell, you'll be able to hear each other's thoughts for a good couple of hours, which, as I understand it, is plenty of time to carry out the assignment," Chris said.

"Absolutely not. I'll do this solo," I said as I leapt to my feet and paced the room. Daniel was the last person I wanted running around inside my head. He was in there enough as it was.

"I'm with Evie on this one. As much as I'd like to go on my first real assignment, I don't think I'm ready for this," Daniel agreed. Shockingly, he didn't have a retort for me for once.

"You're ready." Alex nodded to Daniel before he peered at me over the rim of his glasses. "And this is not a request. It's an order."

Shit.

I looked over at Daniel, and his right leg was bouncing like crazy.

Great, he's probably worried I'll find out he really thinks I'm a world-class bitch.

Suddenly, the back of my neck itched as I recalled some of the thoughts that frequently rolled through my own head where Daniel was concerned. I needed to get a handle on my brain and fast.

Okay, Ev, focus on all the things he does to annoy you, I told myself. God knew there was a laundry list of irritants: *He talks too much. He's cocky, arrogant, and belligerent. He asks too many questions. He has that stupid lopsided grin. His warm skin. The smooth tone of his voice. His laugh. The feel of his breath on the back of my neck. The way the tattoo room fills with the smell of him when he's in it. The way he looks at me when I'm working on him. The way he says my name…*

By the time I'd gotten to the last item on the ever-growing list, I was in my room and didn't even remember walking there.

"I'm so screwed." I slid down the wall and onto the floor.

I poured myself into the shower and tried to get into my pre-assignment routine. I needed to psych myself up; if we had any hopes of pulling this off and coming out the other side alive, I had to be mentally prepared. Not only for what I might inadvertently think about Daniel, but what I might also hear about myself. Did I really want to know what he truly thought about me? I had to face it—I hadn't been the nicest person in the world to him, and most of the time I had done my best to make him feel like shit.

The door opened mid-knock, and Tess poked her head inside. "Hey, are you going to be okay with this?" she asked.

"I don't have much choice, do I?" I shot back. The words came out with a coarse edge, and I could see her face wrinkle with hurt. Jesus, I was acting like a complete asshole. I forced a smile and pulled her out of the doorway and into a hug. "You know me, though. I'll be all right."

"If it makes you feel any better, Chris said Danny went back to his room and threw up," she said as she returned my embrace.

"A little," I laughed.

"Can I ask you something?" she asked tentatively.

"Of course, T. You know you can ask me anything."

"What are you so afraid of?"

"Clowns, puppets, that plastic-headed Burger King guy…"

"Forget it." She shook her head, and turned for the door.

I could have just let her leave, but deep down I knew I would eventually have to come clean, especially with her. Besides, hanging onto that going into an assignment was bad mojo.

"Do you remember Jeremy and Lillian?" I asked before she left the room.

"Yeah, they were here about twenty years ago. She was killed on assignment a few years into their stay here, I think. It was awful, and he was a complete wreck…" She stopped and looked at me. "Sweetie, is that what's keeping you from getting close to anyone? You're afraid to lose them?"

"You didn't see him, Tess," I said as I hugged my arms around my body. "Lana and I were sent to drag him back after he went rogue. It was awful, and I've seen a lot of bad shit, you know that." I remembered the way Jeremy had looked when we'd found him holed up in a shack in Mexicali, just south of the border. His eyes had been flat, emotionless, and he'd had the worst sallow appearance. It was one of the most frightening things I'd ever seen in my hunting career. It hit way too close to home. "I don't want to end up like that or be the cause of anyone else ending up like that."

"You're right, I didn't see *him*, but I saw his handler and hers. Both abandoned, lost, and…" Tess closed her eyes and swallowed hard, clearly trying to keep it together. "I know we joke about what could happen to you out there, but let me tell you something, Evelyn Elizabeth Brighton, there is no one on this earth who will be more devastated than me if anything were to happen to you. Don't you get that?" She grabbed me by the shoulders and gave me a shake and then pointed up at me with one of those bony little fingers of hers. "You listen to me. I know magic, and I will not hesitate to drag your stubborn ass back into this world if you leave it before me. As a matter of fact, you are not *allowed* to leave this world without me, are we clear?"

"Crystal. Thanks, Tess," I said, and we hugged tightly.

"S'what I'm here for, babe."

Daniel and Chris walked into the shop as Tess and I were finishing up the potion mixture. She'd said it would taste like shit, and judging by all the crap that went into it, I could see why. My stomach was churning from the fumes alone. As she continued mixing, Chris stooped down to draw a chalk circle on the floor.

I stepped into the little back room and took my Divinity blade off the wall.

"Be swift, be strong," I whispered to her.

I sensed Daniel enter the room more than heard him, and the blade hummed in my hand in a way she never had before. Not the familiar jolt of power that coursed through me when we faced off with an enemy in battle; no, this was different. It was tender, calming—like she knew him.

"She's beautiful," he said from the doorway. "I'd never seen one in person before. Pictures just don't do a weapon like that justice, in my opinion."

"Amen," I said as I slid my blade into her scabbard. "Are you ready for this?"

"Yeah, but I'd be a liar if I said I wasn't nervous."

"Just don't throw up on me, okay?" I winked.

"Jesus, Chris has a big mouth," he said, scrubbing his hands over his face.

Tess poked her head in and announced, "Saddle up, you two. We're ready."

We stepped out into the main room and saw the circle drawn on the floor. All along the perimeter was the spell, written out in what I assumed was Chris's handwriting because it clearly wasn't T's. She must have really trusted him to have allowed him to write out the incantation for her.

"Take a seat in the center and face each other." Tess took my sword from me, careful to touch only the leather casing. After Daniel and I sat cross-legged on the floor in front of each other, she handed me a pewter cup filled with that nasty-smelling potion. "Take a good swig of this. It's possibly the grossest thing you've ever had in your mouth, but you have to muscle it down. We've got a good amount of bonding agent in here, so the more you drink the longer it will hold."

I rolled my eyes and tipped the cup back, taking a solid gulp. As soon as the viscous liquid hit my tongue, I could feel my throat constrict, refusing to open up and swallow the putrid gunk. I took a few deep breaths through my nose and forced it down. I could practically feel it slide down into my gullet as I gagged and coughed, trying to keep that nasty shit down.

"I hate you," I sputtered as I glared at Tess through one barely open eye.

"I know you do, sugar butt." She patted me on the head. "Next," she announced as she yanked the cup out of my hand and thrust it into Daniel's. I'd noticed that he was already pretty green when he'd walked through the door, but he took the cup and polished off the rest of the potion with a shudder. "All righty, raise your hands, interlock your fingers with each other's, and press your foreheads together."

Raising a suspicious eyebrow at Tess, I crossed my arms over my chest. She *would* find a spell that called for Daniel and me to touch in some way.

"Don't give me your evil-eye-I-don't-think-so face. I do seem to remember a version of this spell that required you both to be completely naked, so either suck it up and hold hands or start stripping, *comprenda?*"

If I knew Tess, she wasn't kidding, and the last thing I wanted to be with Daniel was naked. Well…maybe not the *last* thing. I cleared my throat and raised my hands like a good little hunter.

Daniel rubbed his hands together and wiped them on his jeans before he held them up. His palms were hot when they touched mine, and I could still feel the moisture on them. His tongue darted out and ran over his lips as we leaned our foreheads together.

"Okay, now I need you two to focus," Tess said, and I heard the sound of an old binding cracking as she opened up one of the ancient books.

I had to think—and fast—but my mind was drawing a complete blank. *Think of something, damn it, anything other than how much you want to lean in another few inches and kiss him.*

One thing popped into my head, and I ran with it:

> *'Twas brillig, and the slithy toves*
> *Did gyre and gimble in the wabe;*
> *All mimsy were the borogoves,*
> *And the mome raths outgrabe…*

A poem out of one of my favorite books as a child, *Through the Looking-Glass, and What Alice Found There,* by Lewis Carroll. I knew this story in particular very well because I'd seen my share of real-life Jabberwockies. The sound of Tess's voice drifted into the background as I focused all of my thoughts on the words, reciting the verse in its entirety over and over again.

Then, underneath my own thoughts, creeping into my brain, was another voice that was not my own. A smooth, familiar voice with a baritone timbre—Daniel. It was a soft sound, like he was a million miles away, but as every second passed, his voice became clearer and louder:

> *"Beware the Jabberwock, my son!*
> *The jaws that bite, the claws that catch!*
> *Beware the Jubjub bird, and shun*
> *the frumious Bandersnatch!"*

By the time he'd gotten to the last two words of the verse, it was as if he were speaking out loud, instead of inside my head: "*I remember telling my dad that our neighbor was a Bandersnatch when I was a kid. Turned out he was actually a Lycanter demon.*"

"Is it working? Did it work? Damn it, will someone answer me?" Tess asked as she circled around us in a panic.

I opened my eyes and saw Daniel grinning back at me.

"Okay, I'll admit it first. This is kinda cool," I said.

"It worked! We did it!" Tessa squealed, flinging her arms around Chris's neck and squeezing the crap out of him while she peppered his cheek with kisses.

He blushed furiously as he nodded in agreement but made no attempt to stop her assault.

When at last she released him, Tess explained, "First things first: this isn't an all-access pass into each other's innermost thoughts. With a good amount of tweaking, we were able to create a variation of the original spell that allows you to be able to more or less project the thought to the other person versus having an open line into the other person's head."

"Like a two-way radio?" Daniel asked, picking himself up off of the floor and reaching a hand down to help me up.

"Right." Chris nodded.

"But unlike a walkie-talkie, errant thoughts can seep through, so it is imperative to keep your mind on the mission, even more than normal," Tess clarified.

"Good to know," I said. I grabbed Daniel's hand to stand but released it before I could focus on the feeling of it and risk having a stray thought wander into his brain.

I slipped my arms through the straps of my double-shoulder holster, custom fitted by Isolde with a sheath in the back for my sword, and pulled on my jacket. Effectively concealing our weapons was a big part of the job, especially any time we were in public.

Daniel shoved a clip into one of his revolvers and racked it, pulling the sliding mechanism back and engaging the first bullet, before he set the safety and stuffed it neatly into the holster under his left arm. I always did have a weak spot for a guy with a gun. I quickly turned away and started to gather the necessities for the cloaking spell. Anything to keep my focus off of Daniel and the way he handled a weapon.

"You won't need that. The cloaking spell is built into the mix of the potion, so you guys are good to go," Tess explained.

I took a deep breath and started for the door when T pulled me back and into a tight hug.

"Don't get dead," she whispered, squeezing her arms around my neck.

CHAPTER 7
DANIEL

I tossed on my jacket to conceal my weapons, and Evie and I headed down into the garage, where Josie and Tony were already waiting in a non-descript black van.

"I know it's cliché, but it gets the job done," Josie said from behind the wheel as Evie and I took our seats. "We'll drop you guys off and pick you back up after the mission is complete."

Heading south on a freeway that I couldn't remember the name of, we drove for a good fifteen minutes before I recognized street names like Sunset Boulevard. Josie took the off-ramp from Santa Monica Boulevard and navigated the surface streets with ease.

"These are your panic buttons," Tony explained as he tossed two black boxes back to Evie and me. They were smaller than a key fob and had only one indented button in the middle. "Mash on 'em if you need backup. Josie and I will be out of the demons' sensing range but close enough to swoop in and save your asses if need be." He winked at Evie.

"If I remember right, it was your balls-to-the-wall ass that needed saving not that long ago," Evie said with a quirk of her eyebrow.

"Whatever," Tony huffed, and I shoved the device into my jacket pocket.

Just remember, Evie's voice sounded in my head.

"Shit," I said, fumbling my panic button. It was weird as hell having her voice pop into my head out of nowhere like that, and I accidentally pressed the button, causing Tony's receiver to vibrate across the dashboard.

"Dude?" Tony scrambled to silence the incessant buzzing sound, and Josie snickered.

"I wasn't expecting to hear someone else inside my head yet. It kinda startled me, okay?"

"Rookie," Tony coughed, and Evie rolled her eyes.

You're gonna have to get used to this, she thought to me with a sigh as she pinched the bridge of her nose. *Like I was trying to say, remember that you aren't always going to have your jacket with you, so you might want to put the panic button in something you aren't going to be taking off*. She slid hers into the front pocket of her jeans.

My mind wandered to that tattoo I'd occasionally caught a glimpse of on Evie's lower back as well as the one on the back of her neck.

Keep your mind on the job, her scolding voice reverberated in my head.

I figured she'd only gotten a hint of my wayward mind, though, not the full details, because she wasn't presently trying to beat the shit out of me for thinking about slipping those jeans off of her.

"Sorry." I grinned and leaned back in my seat, slipping the little black box into my front pocket.

"All right, kiddies, this is where you get off," Josie said as she pulled into a parking lot off the main street, parked, and kicked her boots up onto the dashboard.

I looked out of the front window at the grocery store. Evie hopped out and started across the parking lot without even waiting for me. Catching up with her easily, I followed her lead and headed out with her onto the sidewalk past the store.

"Where are we going?" I asked, following her down the sidewalk to the block behind the market. It was strange how neighborhoods, especially in major cities, could go from nice and decent to really shitty and kinda scary in a block or two.

Evelyn cut me a quick glare and tapped her temple. *Quiet, damn it*, she thought. *We're heading to their nest*. She pointed to a tall and probably abandoned apartment complex. *They're in there, and we're getting close to their sound range. It's imperative that you keep your focus. Thoughts* only *from here on out, got it?*

Got it. Damn, sorry, I didn't—

Don't be sorry. Just don't do it again.

As we got closer to our destination, the number of homeless vagrants and junkies increased. Typical, not only for a demon nest but any abandoned city building. I kept my mind and my mouth shut until we reached the back of the old apartment building.

Stay here, and on my signal, slip out of your jacket and quickly toss it to me. Got it? she asked when we stepped through the door. The thought process of what she was planning continued to seep into my head as she made her way into the rundown lobby and toward the back, where two men slept.

In complete knee-jerk reaction, I started to answer her. Luckily, before I could get a word out, Evie's finger was over my lips.

I swear, your mouth is going to be the death of me, she thought with a glare.

You're not the first woman to tell me that, I responded with a wink and slid my tongue between my lips, licking the end of her finger.

She jerked her hand away and wiped it on her jeans. *You're disgusting.*

That's just what your conscious mind says. But your unconscious mind on the other hand…

Goddamn it, would you focus! Her voice ricocheted off my cranium and bounced around inside my skull. *On my signal, got it?* she reiterated.

I nodded, indicating that her words were heard loud and clear.

Moving with the stealth of a jungle cat, she snatched a small item from one of the men and discretely placed it into the other man's hand. She retraced her steps until she was in position next to the first vagrant; she nudged him with her foot, waking him. The man stirred and spied one of his "prized possessions" in the hands of the other bum. He wailed as he hurdled himself at the second man, resulting in an extremely loud scuffle.

Now! Evie thought as she whipped her leather jacket off and tucked it into the top of what used to be tenant mailboxes. That, of course, exposed her weapons, making them easier to access.

I followed her instructions and tossed her my own brown leather coat for safekeeping.

As the bum ruckus subsided, Evie quickly pulled her sword off of her back and nodded up the stairway.

You know, I love seeing a hot chick with a sword as much as the next guy, but I read somewhere that, in recent months, some demons have come up that are immune to the Divinity sword's powers.

You know what I read? she replied. *That one-in-three unfocused rookies eat it on their first assignments.*

I was just trying to be helpful.

Then shut up and focus.

Harpy.

I heard that, she thought as she silently moved up the steps of the filthy, graffiti-riddled stairwell.

You were supposed to.

Evie shook her head, and I saw her grinning when she turned on the landing and headed up the next flight. On reaching the next landing, we were bombarded with a putrid stench, the kind that catches in the back of your throat and sticks to the surface of your tongue.

Jesus, what the hell is that smell? I asked, fighting back the immense urge to gag.

Limaske demons lay down their musk as an offensive mechanism, she explained. *It creates an invisible wall of sorts. The scent causes the intruder to cough and gag, alerting the demons and giving them a chance to escape.*

Or feed, I added as I stepped over the skeletal remains of a human being.

That too, so watch your ass and try not to make any involuntary gagging sounds. If you can muscle down that swill Tess made us drink without blinking, you can do this.

As we reached the top of the next landing, we saw three distinct nests. Thin, lime-green wisps with the consistency of spun glass clung to the ceiling, walls, and the sides of their fibrous, husk-like nests. Hanging on the wall from big metal hooks were what looked to be flesh-colored jumpsuits.

They wear those out in public to conceal themselves, Evie explained as I eyed one of the jumpers.

They look like they're made out of real human skin, I said, noting what looked to be arm hair on the one in front of me.

They are.

Very Buffalo Bill.

Quid pro quo, Clarice, she responded, clearly getting the *Silence of the Lambs* reference as she stepped up to one of the nests. *Once we start this, it's going to happen very fast. You need to keep on your toes. Are you ready?* She drew her sword across her palm, breaking the skin enough to spill her blood and bring the Divinity blade to its full power.

Ready as I'll ever be, I responded as my hands wrapped around the grips of the set of twin Smith and Wesson 945 performance pistols. Yeah, I was ready.

Evie sliced open the side of the nest, and a dead human body slid out in place of a sleeping demon. Before her thoughts or mine could process that this was a trap, I saw a demon face appear from the fibers covering the ceiling, ready to drop behind her.

I tugged my weapon out of the holster as I watched Evie arch her sword behind her head and effectively lodge it into that of the crouching beast. The magic in the blade cut through its otherworldly skull like it was butter. The glow from her tattoos and markings on her bare arms lit up the dark, dank room, not to mention the energy that pulsed and illuminated underneath her white tank top. She was our flashlight.

Another demon dropped for a split second to hiss at us before launching itself back into the hairy ceiling and disappearing. A third rumbled down the stairs from the upper floor and headed straight for Evie.

This one was slightly different, though. It was clearly of Limaske origin, but it was larger than the other two in musculature and stature. Even its skin had an odd appearance to it, a vaguely purple hue to the normally dingy blue tint.

"Evelyn, wait!" I shouted, but her sword was already in motion.

The mighty, magical blade bounced off the demon flesh like it was nothing more than a plastic toy.

"What the fu…" she said as she whacked at it again only to make a thwacking sound against the tough, unnatural hide.

The demon laughed and brushed its arm as if Evie's attacks had been nothing but a bothersome insect before it reared a claw back to strike.

Everything was happening wicked-fast—Evie had no time to reach her backup revolver, and I could feel something approach me from behind. I had to either whirl around, sink the beast behind me, and pray I'd have enough time left to take out the one about to relieve Evie of her head or take care of her situation first.

It wasn't a hard decision.

I aimed quickly and squeezed off the first round, obliterating the big bastard's hand into nothing more than a bloody stump before I pulled the trigger a second time and popped one round into its left eyeball.

Then it was like I was in a dream or one of those movies where everything happens in super-slow motion, because as the unholy, lifeless body sank to the ground in front of Evie, I felt talons digging into my shoulder and the upper half of my body being arched back. I could hear the sticky sound of jaws opening and smell brimstone and the rotten stench of demon breath as the creature behind me exhaled with a hiss.

I could also hear something else in the back of my mind, a whir-ring sound, almost—wait, no—words, a voice. Evie's voice, rattling through a series of equations and statistics at an ungodly speed and, underneath all of the ramblings, a tiny plea: *I need him.*

Something whizzed through my hair just before I heard the crack of a gun, and the next thing I knew, the grip the creature'd had on me was gone and I was covered in slimy demon blood. I stood up straight and wiped the viscous liquid and bits of brain matter off my face.

"Oh gross, it got in my mouth. Ugh, it tastes like that God-awful smell. Thanks, by the way," I spat and gagged as I reached up and pulled shards of demon bone and a tooth or two out of my hair.

"Yeah, well, a demon dies, all I have to do is check a box. *You* die, and I have to fill out a shit-load of paperwork." She slid her sword into its sheath on her back and looked at the dead beast at her feet. "Z and Finn are going to want to take a look at this joker. How did you know my blade wouldn't work on it anyway?" she asked as she shoved the body with her foot.

"He looked different than the others."

"Good eye," she acknowledged, and she made her way around the room, taking a mental note, it seemed, of everything in there. We cautiously wandered the rest of the building as we waited for the cleanup crew.

After it arrived, we made our way back down to the main floor, retrieved our jackets out of the old mailbox unit, and headed back out into civilization. As we left, Evie explained that our pick-up destination would be different than our drop-off point: Bianca's Deli off of Vermont Avenue, because Tony liked their homemade baklava.

We started to walk west along the world-famous Sunset Boulevard, and I noticed Evie's voice become more distant inside my head. I opened my mouth to mention it when we walked into—and suddenly passed through—what I could only describe as a force field. No sooner had we breached the barrier than every head on the street turned our way. Evie stopped short, and I nearly walked into the back of her.

"Back up." She reached back, pressing her palm against my stomach to gently shove me in the opposite direction. "Back up now." Her pushing became urgent when the people started turning in our direction. My back hit the barrier, and it felt immensely stronger than when we'd inadvertently passed through it before. It was like a giant wall of cellophane.

"I can't get out," I said, pressing my shoulders against the invisible resistance to get it to give way.

"*G'tihl ni'eth kard, vieg ot'ema krasp,*" she whispered under her breath, and her hand heated up so much it practically burned my skin through my T-shirt.

My instinct was to go for my gun and protect us while Evie worked her spell, but as we were out in public, that probably wasn't the best idea unless we had no other option. The barrier shifted slightly, and I remembered something Tess had flagged in one of the magic books she'd given me to read: if I concentrated and opened my mind, Evie could tap into my magic abilities.

I also remembered reading something about skin-on-skin contact; it might have been a different spell, but I wasn't about to take any chances. Swiftly working my hands up underneath the hem of her shirt, I placed my palms on the bare skin just above her hips. It was warm, smooth, and tingled with magic. I needed something to anchor my focus, and I chose her flesh or, more so, the energy I could feel coursing through it.

Evie's voice picked up in speed and volume, and the connection inside our minds flickered. She knew what I was doing, and it was working. My foot made it out of the bubble of evil, and I planted it against the concrete, gaining a bit of leverage.

Gritting my teeth as I wrapped my entire arm around Evie's waist, I heaved with all my might to fling her a few feet free of the barrier and worked my own way out. I'd always heard the term "hit the ground running" but had never actually seen it until I watched Evie lurch forward sprinting as soon as her boots made contact with the sidewalk, and I was two steps behind her.

She whipped her cell phone out of her pocket. "We need a pick-up on the fly, right now," she yelled into the receiver as she ran. "Southeast on Sunset en route to Fountain Avenue."

We raced, balls out, down the street. Being larger than her, I could have easily passed her, but I kept the same pace. The sound of a roaring engine and series of horn honks announced Josie and Tony's arrival. The big black van slowed in front of us but didn't stop, and I saw the back doors fly open. I sped in front of Evie and grabbed onto one of them, getting a good grip before I turned back to reach for her. As I wrapped my hand around her wrist, ready to yank her into the van, I peeked over her shoulder to see about four demons of varying breeds closing in fast.

"Holy shit, Evelyn, jump!" I yelled with a good, swift yank.

Her body sailed past my head, and I was almost immediately hauled into the back of the van myself, landing right on top of her.

The van doors slammed closed, and the vehicle launched into high speed, leaving our pursuers in our wake. Josie made a sharp U-turn, and Evie and I rolled across the floor. As she hovered over me, she looked to my hand, which I'd pressed against the wall of the van to stop us from crashing into it, and I had a flickering insight into her mind. One last burst of thought before the line connecting our consciousnesses was turned off for good. It wasn't even a thought, really; it was more like a feeling than anything else.

She liked the way my hands had felt on her bare skin.

I opened my mouth to say something. Hell, I almost pulled that cheesy-ass brush-the-girl's-hair-behind-her-ear thing you always see guys do in chick flicks. And honestly, if she hadn't made such a sour face at the thought, I might have gone full wine-and-cheese right there in the back of that weird-smelling van in front of Tony and Josie.

Evie's eyes met mine, and they softened for a split second like she wanted to say something to me.

"Wooo!" Tony whooped as he walloped Evie hard on a butt cheek. "Now *that* is what I call a rescue! You done good, newbie." He reached over and ruffled my hair.

"Thanks," I said unappreciatively, shooting him a glare for his shitty timing.

"Whoa, someone's bitchy post-assignment," he mumbled as he ambled up to the passenger seat.

"You're bleeding," Evie said, and she sat up and pulled my jacket away from my left shoulder. She tore my T-shirt open at the neck and exposed three distinct puncture wounds from the demon's claws. Leaning over, she reached under the seat, pulled out a black satchel, and began rifling through its contents. "That was really stupid, you know."

"What?" I asked, suddenly feeling lightheaded. I tried to blink the woozy feeling away, but all that did was make me nauseated. "What the hell's happening?"

"Drive faster," Evelyn barked to Josie as she yanked a packet out of the black canvas bag, and after ripping it open with her teeth, poured its powdery contents onto my shoulder. It hurt like a son of a bitch, and I grunted with pain. "Why didn't you tell me you were hurt? The cleanup crew could have treated you on-scene." She pressed a big square of gauze onto the wound, which made it hurt even more.

"It's just a scratch…Jesus, I think I'm going to throw up." I groaned through gritted teeth.

"Scratch, my ass. Drink this." Lifting my head, she tilted a bottle to my lips. "Stupid rookie, you're damn lucky you aren't dead right now," she said as I took a good gulp of the salty liquid.

Once the potion hit my stomach, my head started to clear and I instinctively tried to sit up only to have Evie shove me back down.

"Be still. The elixir is only a stabilizer. You need to stay calm and move as little as possible. Limaske claws are poisonous enough to make you sick with just a scratch, and these are pretty deep."

I looked down at my shoulder and saw green streaks radiating out from every puncture in my flesh.

"When we ran from those other demons, it pulled the poison into your bloodstream faster than normal. But if you would have said something before, you could have been inoculated onsite and avoided all this," Evie said.

"I counted about four different species of demons coming after you guys," Josie said as she hit the freeway on-ramp like it was a launching pad. "That is so weird; they generally don't intermingle like that."

"I know," Evie responded, and she pulled out another unopened packet of gauze and held it between her teeth while she shook up a bottle of liquid. "Now this is gonna hurt." Tearing open the package, she covered a section of gauze with the blue fluid.

When she touched the compress to my skin, I wailed a slew of obscenities and my back arched off the van floor in pain.

"I'm sorry," she whispered.

That was the last thing I remember hearing before I lost consciousness.

I woke up in the infirmary with an IV in my right arm and Isolde tending to my shoulder.

"There you are. You had us a little worried, Daniel. It's good to have you back," she said with a smile.

"Finally," Evie said, yawning. "Now maybe I can go back to my room and get some sleep." I turned my head and saw her stretching in a chair on the other side of my bed. She still had on the same clothes she'd worn before, with her sword and gun in their respective holsters and placed neatly on top of her folded jacket on the unoccupied bed next to me.

"How long have I been out?" I asked.

"A good four or five hours," Isolde said, pulling off the bandage and tossing it into a wastebasket next to the bed. I glanced over and saw multiple discarded bandages covered in what looked like green blood, except the last one, which was bright red. She prodded around on my shoulder, and I winced at the sharp pain. "Looks excellent. We can put some salve on it now."

"Okay, well, now that you're alive and shit, I'll go get Papa Bear. He's going to want to be debriefed on that 'magic bubble' or whatever that was we stumbled into." It was about that time that I realized Evie was touching my leg — my shin, actually — unconsciously stroking it back and forth through the sheet as she spoke. "I'm gonna grab Tess too; she should be part of anything pertaining to magic." She gave the top of my foot a reassuring pat before heading out the door.

"Is she always like that?" I asked Isolde when I was sure Evie was gone. "So —" I tried to think of a delicate way to say cold and distant but just couldn't seem to come up with anything nicer than that "—ya know…"

"Yes, I know, but Evelyn does have her moments." She smiled and nodded to the spot on my leg that Evie had just touched.

"She confuses me," I confessed. Something about Isolde made me feel warm and comfortable enough to open up to her. Besides, I had a feeling she'd known Evie for quite a few years. "Half the time I think she hates my guts and that I'm more of a nuisance than anything else."

"And the other half of the time?" Isolde asked with a grin as she taped a fresh bandage over my wound.

I shrugged my good shoulder, uncertain of how to answer that.

"I see." Isolde nodded knowingly with a spark in her eye. "Sit up."

I slowly leaned forward in the bed, and she wrapped a thick elastic ACE bandage around my shoulder.

"Be patient with her. Evelyn has been around for…*some time,* and that tends to make one set in one's ways." She wound the cloth under my arm and over again.

I sat and thought about what Isolde had said as she finished bandaging me up. I wanted to ask her more, but before I could, Evie had returned with Alex, Tess, and Chris. We chronicled everything that had happened from the moment we'd left the van to the moment we'd returned to it. Tess took furious notes and asked about a million questions about the "magic bubble" thing. She seemed intently intrigued if not pissed that whoever was running the show in there had been able to keep things under wraps without being detected.

When Isolde deemed it time, she shooed everyone out of the infirmary and told me to get some rest as she injected something for the pain into my IV that made my head swim.

During the night, Isolde would rouse me to check my vitals and assess the wound, and in my drugged-out haze, I saw Evie slumped over in the chair next to my bed, wearing Hello Kitty pajamas. I laughed to myself at the hallucination before drifting back to sleep.

Chapter 8
EVELYN

Being drained after a big assignment was normal, so it was no surprise that I fell asleep in the chair in the infirmary. However, I freaked out when I woke up leaning on the side of Daniel's bed and found myself practically nose to nose with him, one hand curled around his and the other slung up over the pillow and playing with a lock of his hair. I leapt up out of the chair, and it made a God-awful noise as its feet skidded against the linoleum.

Daniel stirred in his sleep, and I immediately froze where I stood. I didn't dare breathe or blink until he settled again, which he did fairly quickly. Thank God. Honestly, I don't know what I would have done if he *had* woken up and caught me practically curled up in bed with him.

It was five thirty in the morning, and nearly everyone in the house should have been getting up right about then, so I was lucky to find the basement hallways empty. After sneaking out of the infirmary and up the stairs without being detected, I peeked around the corner into the kitchen, the only route to the upper level of the house, and saw Isolde busy futzing with something on the stove. Her back was to me, and I had to make a decision to either slink back downstairs or make a break for it. Gathering all my stealthy abilities, I took a few tentative steps.

"Is Daniel still asleep?" Isolde asked before I could get to the kitchen table; she didn't even have to turn around to know I was there.

"Umm…yeah?" I could have lied and said I didn't know, I suppose, and if it had been anyone else, even Alex or Tess, I probably would have. But not Isolde; I could never lie to her.

"Well, we'll let him rest for a little while longer, then. Eat up and take it easy today. You had a big day yesterday, and I know you couldn't have slept well in that chair all night long." She grinned as she slid an avocado and bacon omelet onto a plate and set it on the counter in front of me.

"Yeah, uh, about that," I said, poking my breakfast with my finger.

"Don't worry, your secret is safe with me," she whispered as she handed me a fork, kissed me on the forehead, and plopped a huge dollop of sour cream onto the top of the omelet.

I finished my breakfast, and Isolde promptly handed me a tray of food to take down to Daniel. I tried my damnedest to get out of it by convincing her she needed to check his vitals, but she wasn't having it. She held out the tray of food, insisting with that warm smile of hers and a mischievous twinkle in her eye. Behind all of Isolde's Suzy Homemaker and Florence Nightingale tendencies, there was a bit of gypsy in her, and it wouldn't have surprised me in the least if she had a crystal ball up in her room somewhere.

"Fine," I groaned as I took the tray. While I couldn't refuse anything she asked me to do, I didn't have to be happy about it.

The silverware clinked against the plate as I walked down the hall. I stopped outside of the infirmary room door, but leaning against the wall, I could still hear the clinking and realized it was because I was trembling.

Jesus Christ, Ev, pull yourself together! He's just a cocky, pain-in-the-ass rookie. The sooner you train him, the sooner he'll be out of your hair. And your dreams. And nearly every waking thought…

But I don't want him to leave.

That thought scared the crap out of me.

With a deep breath, I shoved the door open with my shoulder, my you-do-absolutely-nothing-for-me, "Serious Evelyn" face screwed on tight. He was still asleep and looked so serene; his naked chest and shoulders peeked out from the top of the crisp white bed sheet. The one lock of hair I'd been playing with earlier lay curled against his smooth forehead, and his lips were pressed together in a natural curve that made him look like he was smiling at a dream. Maybe he was. His skin was paler than usual, but that was more than likely due to the poisoning. Even with that, he was still exceptionally beautiful. I stood and stared for God knows how long, watching him sleep, before I set the tray of food onto the table next to his bed and checked the monitor he was attached to and the level of fluid in his IV bag.

"Are those Hello Kitty pajamas?"

Whirling around, I saw Daniel staring up at me, wearing that damn smirk.

"Yes, why?" I asked, suddenly very self-conscious about my appearance for probably the first time in my life. I looked horrid, like I'd slept in a chair all night. Oh wait, I had.

"I just didn't peg you as a Hello Kitty type of chick. It's cute. I like 'em," he said, reaching out and flicking the side of my pink lounge pants.

"Tony got them for me for Christmas." I tugged at the tiny pajama tee and crossed my arms over my chest, wishing like hell I had grabbed my robe before I'd come down the night before. Tony *would* buy something that hugged my boobs like a second skin. "I brought you something to eat." I nodded to the tray on the bedside table, my hands still tucked tightly under my arms.

Daniel sat up and hissed in pain as he tried to reach for his breakfast.

"Sorry, I'll get that. Isolde should be by in a little bit to check your shoulder and put a fresh dressing on it."

"Thanks," he said, smiling as I set the tray in his lap —not that smarmy grin that made me want to punch him in the throat, but a warm, genuine smile that turned my insides to Jell-O.

"Evelyn," Isolde's voice said through the intercom, jolting me back into reality.

I practically ran over to the intercom box on the wall and pressed the button.

"Yeah?"

"Would you do me a favor and take a peek at Daniel's wounds? Oh, and put a fresh bandage on them as well, please. I can't quite get away from the kitchen at the moment."

"Sure, I guess."

"Wonderful. You know where the supplies are, and go ahead and hang a fresh IV bag; the one on there should be about empty," she said.

"No problem, Iz. I'll take care of it."

I'd noticed that the IV bag was low when I had looked at it earlier and was going to change it before Daniel had startled me. We had a mini hospital down here and could handle about any kind of situation that we might find ourselves in. Let's face it, Cedars Sinai or the UCLA Medical Center weren't exactly equipped to handle Limaske demon poisoning and the like. I gathered fresh bandages and a new IV bag out of the medical closet while Daniel ate. When he was finished, I removed the ACE bandage around his shoulder and let him lie back in the bed as I carefully peeled the tape off of the wound dressing. I had to really concentrate to keep my fingers from trembling, which was odd; I'd touched his bare flesh before when I'd tattooed him.

But now it seemed somehow different.

If he hadn't taken out that demon the way he had, I would be in a box — or two — on my way to the Lebriga main offices overseas. He'd saved my life, almost at the cost of his own.

"Can I tell you something?" I asked as I pulled off the old dressing.

"Yeah, of course," he said.

"You smell really, really bad."

Daniel laughed so hard he pulled his shoulder for the second time that morning.

"I'm just saying, you might want to pop into the bathroom and take care of some stuff before I bandage you back up again."

"Are you offering to give me a sponge bath?" he asked with that absurd-but-starting-to-grow-on-me smirk.

Say no.

"Ew, and no, everything you need is in there. Just be careful of your shoulder, okay?" I threw a washcloth at his head.

"Last chance," he said as he stood in the bathroom doorway, wiggling his eyebrows before he disappeared behind the door.

I busied myself changing the bed sheets and double-checking the bandaging supplies, anything to keep my mind off the fact that Daniel was ten feet away, behind that door. Naked. Soapy, wet, and naked.

"Evie?" his voice called from the other side of the door.

"Ye—" My voice crackled like a prepubescent, twelve-year-old boy, and I quickly cleared my throat. "Yeah?"

"I need a little help in here."

"I'll bet you do. Nice try, perv," I shot back.

"No, seriously, I can't reach around the right side of my back. I have pants on, I swear."

I stood and stared at the white door.

What are you so worried about? He has pants on, for God's sake. Pull yourself together.

I reached up under my hair for the tattoo on the back of my neck; the ink burned at the base of my skull and under my fingertips. In the years that I'd carried this mark on my flesh, it had warmed and cast a faint light but never as bright or hot as it did when I was around Daniel.

Taking a deep breath to calm my nerves, I walked across the room and gripped the door handle. Holy crap, I was more nervous about this than going into a demon nest.

When I opened the door, he was struggling to get his pants on straight, using only one hand and not doing a very good job. The waistband was folded over onto itself about three times in the back, making it nearly impossible to get the pants up correctly. They were pulled up crooked, and the top of his ass crack was showing. It looked like he'd been dressed by a drunk.

"Christ, you're a mess. How much pain medication are you on?"

"Ha-ha, smart ass. A little help here?" he asked as he tugged the waistband with one hand.

Remember, Ev, you're pulling the pants UP, I told myself. Easily sliding my thumbs under the waistband, I carefully unrolled the elastic, and when smoothing it out, my fingertips grazed the top curve of his butt before I pulled the pants up over his navel.

"Easy. Little Danny and the boys need some breathing room!" he hollered as he stepped back, tugging the pants down about two inches.

"Sorry." I moved around behind him, trying not to think about Daniel's various parts, little or otherwise. Eager to get him out of the confines of the bathroom as fast as I could, I quickly swiped the soapy washcloth over his back.

The close proximity in the small room rapidly became overwhelming. He didn't say anything to me as I finished washing his back or even afterward when I helped him pull the sheet over his legs and set to bandaging his shoulder. He just watched every move I made, and I found myself working slowly and carefully because I didn't want to cause him any undue pain. But to be honest, it was mainly because I liked the way it felt when he watched me. It thrilled me and made me nervous at the same time.

I had to get out of there.

"Okay, you're all set," I said as I gave his vitals one last check.

"How long do you think I'll be locked up in here?"

"Isolde should be in soon to give you an official once-over, but you're healing up nicely, so you should be back out in the general population later today if I had to guess." I gave his leg a reassuring pat. When I turned for the door, Daniel quickly grabbed me by the hand and pulled me closer, utilizing strength I didn't think he still had after having been attacked. My heart hammered like crazy inside my chest, and my mouth suddenly went very dry.

"Thank you…for everything," he said as he raised my hand to his mouth and placed a gentle kiss on my skin. His lips were warm, soft and felt far better in real life than anything I had conjured up in my imagination.

I stood there stunned for a moment, my mouth hanging open.

"You're welcome," I managed to croak out, yanking my hand free and bolting for the door before I could utter anything ridiculously idiotic or worse.

I raced down the hall and up the stairs to my room like I was being chased by the biggest, baddest demon. Luckily, there was no one in my path to question why I hauled ass, especially Tess; the explanation would have been extremely awkward. By the time I reached my bedroom and whipped the door open, I was sucking air pretty hard.

Making a beeline for the bathroom, I slammed the door shut behind me; my fingers trembled as I fumbled to turn the lock on the knob. I stripped off my pajamas, crawled into the shower, and sank to the floor. The water rushed over my head and trickled down my back as I sat under the spray. With rivulets rolling along my spine, all I could think about was the one lone droplet of water I'd watched trickle down between Daniel's shoulder blades. How it moved over his skin, followed the natural muscle tone, and left a shimmering trail until it disappeared, soaking into the waistband of his pants.

What the hell was happening to me? I wasn't this girl. I didn't fawn over men or have those repugnant feelings of gooey love and shit like that. I'd been around for a long time, and I knew that the real world didn't allow things like that to happen.

Or did it?

I thought about Alex and Isolde and Tony and Josie. Were they the anomalies here because they made it work with what we did, or was I too afraid to try and to risk winding up like Jeremy and Lillian?

I was so wrapped up in my own thoughts as I turned off the water that even the light knock on the bathroom door startled me.

"Ev, you okay in there?" Josie asked. "I saw you run out of the infirmary."

Great, I thought as I quickly dried off. "Did anyone else see?" I grabbed my robe off the hook and slipped it on.

"No, I don't think so. I was coming in from the garage, and you looked upset. Do you need me to kick Danny's ass or something? I don't give a shit if he's injured. I'll bring the beat down on him," she said.

"No, but thanks," I said, chuckling as I pulled the door open. I tried to pretend that everything was fine, that *I* was fine as I grabbed some clothes out of my closet and started tugging them on.

Josie wasn't buying it. She just stood there outside the bathroom door with her brightly colored arms crossed. I was particularly proud of the work I'd done on her, weaving her incantations into vibrant works of art. There were tropical flowers, butterflies, and elaborate fighting fish, even a zombie pin-up girl with a brain on a platter on her right shoulder — that one was my favorite.

"Look, I know Tess is generally your go-to gal for this kind of thing, and if you want me to go get her I will, but you have to talk to someone or it's gonna eat you up."

Burying my head in my sock drawer, I acted like I didn't hear her, but as soon as I chanced a look up and saw the way she stared at me, I realized she wasn't going to let this go. I fiddled with my socks and figured the best route to take was the straight one; I wasn't a beat-around-the-bush kind of girl and everyone knew it.

"How did you know, with Tony, I mean?" I asked, not really sure if I wanted to be asking this or not.

She smiled wide and shook her head. I think she was even blushing.

"It's beyond corny," she laughed. "Tony and I had been having sex for months, blowing off steam after assignments and just keeping it casual, ya know? Sort of a friends-with-benefits kinda thing, except I couldn't stand him. Until one afternoon we were on a mission in Chinatown, trying to get information from an informant in the Mogwai district, and it got hairy. As you know, we barely managed to get out of there with our asses intact." She looked down at her hands as she remembered the events. "When we got back to the house, Tony pulled me out of the car before the garage door had finished closing all the way. He didn't say anything, didn't crack a joke or flash those ridiculous dimples at me; he just grabbed me, harder than he ever had before, leaned down, and kissed me for the first time."

"Wait, you two slept together for months before you ever kissed?"

"Of course. It was just sex, Evie, a means to an end," she said. "Don't get me wrong, it was phenomenal. You know how that post-assignment, raw, animal sex is?"

I nodded and couldn't help the eye roll that accompanied it. Yes, I did in fact know — that one night with Z was right up there in my top three best sexcapades ever. If I'm honest, we probably would have still been having great sex if he hadn't tried to make it something more than what it was: mind-numbing and precisely what Josie had said, a means to an end.

"I had cursed Tony and those damn dimples of his every day since he'd sauntered through our door, but after that moment in the garage, I knew I'd never kiss another man for the rest of my life."

"Ugh, I was afraid you were going to say something like that," I moaned, pulling at my hair.

"Jesus, what the hell did he do to you in there, anyway?"

"He said thank you."

Later in the day, I lay back in my bed, stared at the ceiling, and contemplated what the hell I was going to do. This was new ground for me, all these gooey emotions that I'd never had any use for before running around in my head and making me stupid.

Right on cue, Tess breezed through the door and plopped down next to me.

"Convinced yet?" she asked casually.

"Of what?"

I could hear the frustration in the enormous breath she let out.

"Okay, let's pretend that I don't know anything. Pretend I don't know you from Adam and I have no clue what you want or what I'm convinced is going to happen when the dust settles. How does he make you feel?"

Annoyed, aggravated, excited, elated, confident, nervous, confused…

"Like someone scooped out my brain, ran it through a blender, and poured it back into my skull," I said. I took a deep breath and did my best to prepare myself for what I was about to say next. "I spent all last night in the infirmary watching him sleep."

There, I'd finally admitted it. Out loud. To another person.

Tess was quiet for a moment, which was highly unusual. Normally she would have been bouncing on the bed shouting, "I told you so!" at me or something equally as annoying. But she didn't; she just lay there and nodded.

"I don't have to explain myself to Chris. He just understands me on some cosmic, otherworldly level," she finally said.

"Well, that's kinda scary," I teased, poking her in the ribs with my elbow.

"I know, right?" She giggled, and we both flew into a fit of laughter. "He kissed me last night," she said when the silliness died down.

"How was it?" I asked eagerly. The question surprised even me as the words flew out of my mouth before I could catch them.

"Warm, like fresh peach cobbler." She smiled.

I'd known Tess longer than any other living creature and had heard her talk about kissing guys for the better part of a century. But I'd never seen her smile like that. What she'd found in Chris was real.

"Shit," I groaned as I slung my pillow over my face.

"You know what you have to do, don't you?"

"Yes," I said from underneath the pillow.

Yes, I did know. It was fairly evident based on talking to Josie, and now, after this, it was pretty clear what needed to happen…

I'm going to have to kiss Daniel. Crap.

CHAPTER 9
DANIEL

I stared at the spot where Evelyn had been standing two seconds before, wondering what in the hell I'd done to make her bolt like that. The immediate sense of loss I'd felt the moment she'd yanked her hand out of mine was worse than the full effects of the Limaske poisoning. What was it about her that had crawled down into me and latched itself onto my insides? She was everywhere—in my brain, in my heart, in my very soul—and there wasn't a damned thing I could do about it, no matter how badly she treated me. I tried like hell to fight it, but as soon as I realized that I hadn't been hallucinating, that Evie *did* wear Hello Kitty pajamas and made little noises in her sleep, I knew it was a battle I wasn't going to win.

About an hour later, Isolde stopped in like Evie had said she would and gave me the all-clear to leave the infirmary. She said I'd have to take it easy for a few days, which meant no going rounds with Evie in the ring. I was disappointed to hear that, but at least that would give me some time to wrap my head around my feelings.

"Mornin' sunshine," Chris crowed as he walked in with a fresh set of clothes for me, tossing them onto the bed. "Get dressed; there's a house meeting in the conference room. Z's back with some serious intel."

After I pulled my clothes on with some assistance from Chris, we headed out into the hall and down to the conference room. Nearly everyone was seated by the time we made it there, and we all looked like King Arthur and his knights sitting around the giant oak table in the middle of the room. No sooner had Chris and I settled into our chairs than Evie and Tess breezed in and sat across the table.

Glancing up, I felt the air whoosh out of my lungs. Evelyn looked amazing, like I'd never seen her before. Her hair wasn't tied back in a braid as per her usual. Instead, it flowed freely over her shoulders and down her back. She looked directly at me, and I waved, like a dork, but it was worth it to see a grin on her face as she shook her head at me.

"Good afternoon, everyone," Alex said. "Zachary has done an excellent job gathering information from the otherworld sources he's acquired in a timely manner." He nodded to Z, who stood to his full height.

"Aremoc. That's this demon clan's moniker, and they are the manipulators of manipulators. Word is, they've convinced at least three other clans to join in their cause, and they're trying to gain more allies—more specifically, the Mogwai clan in Chinatown."

"Holy shit," Tony said next to me.

"That's not all. My sources tell me that, amongst other methods that are still unclear, they've figured out how to get around weaknesses of certain breeds by forcing evolution through some kind of dark magic."

"Like the Divinity blade immunity," I said, remembering the way Evie's sword had had no effect on the big Limaske demon.

"Exactly. I've heard of their leader, Mzetir, and he is working some very new, very dark magic," Alex said.

"So what does this clown want? Do we even know yet?" Tony asked.

"Everything, from what I can gather," Z answered. "This joker has something to prove, a real sense of entitlement too. He actually believes that we've ruled the roost for long enough and it's their turn to run things around here, and he's seriously hell-bent on making it happen."

"Making *what* happen?" Evie asked.

"Taking over control of Los Angeles," Alex replied.

"Holy shit," Tony repeated as he sank back in his chair.

"What about that bubbly force-fieldy thing? Did you find out anything about that?" Tess asked anxiously.

"Yeah, it works like a containment field. They've enveloped pretty much everything between Sunset and Hollywood, out to where Ev and Danny ran into it, and as far east as Vine. They've taken over everything inside, and as I understand it, have turned the W Hotel into their headquarters," Zach said.

"We have to get in there," Evie and I both said at the same time.

"*You* aren't going anywhere," Evie stated, pointing her finger at me.

"What? That's bullshit! I pulled your ass out of that thing, remember?"

"And you nearly died, goddamn it!" she yelled, pounding the table in front of her, her jaw clenched tight.

"Stop," Alex commanded, planting his hands firmly on the table. "Nobody is going anywhere."

Don't, Evelyn mouthed, shaking her head as she glared across the table at me, her bottom lip trembling ever so slightly.

"If I recall, that force field stripped both of you of any magic. Until we can remedy that, neither of you is going anywhere near that thing, do you understand?" he asked.

"But—" Evie started to protest.

"No, that is a direct order from corporate," Alex said sternly, slapping a file down onto the table. Most of the words on it were obscured with Post-Its and other notations, but one thing was clear at the bottom of the top page: a *G* in elaborate, old-world script.

G. The big guy. Mr. Lebriga himself. This was serious shit.

"Yes, sir." Evelyn nodded obediently. "What can we do, then?"

"First, Tessa, I need you to work on a spell, a potion, an anything that will hold inside that force field. Christopher will accompany you and assist in any way needed."

"Got it," Tess replied as she hurried out of the room and into her shop, Chris two steps behind her.

"Second, whatever Tessa concocts is going to have to be field tested," he continued. Evelyn and I both moved to stand, ready to take on our assignment. "Not you two. Zachary, take Anthony and

Josephine for some more reconnaissance. Try to figure out a relatively safe spot that we can use for testing when Tessa has something solid."

Tony, Josie, and Z all left with their respective handlers in tow.

"How soon can she begin his next marking, and when can he get back to his training?" Alex asked Isolde, who was standing near the door, waiting for instruction.

She hemmed and hawed for a moment before she spoke. "He should be healed enough for marking by tomorrow, but no ring time for another three days at least." Her warm brown eyes shifted from Evie to me and back again. "Until then, studies only, and bring him into the infirmary later this evening so I can check his healing progress, understood?"

"Yes, Isolde." Evie nodded.

"These are the known demon clans associated with the Aremoc; make sure he is well versed," Alex said after he jotted something down on a piece of paper and handed it to Evelyn.

"Yes, sir." She took the paper. She gave it a quick glance before she looked to me. "Come on. We've got a lot of work to do."

We headed down to Z and Finn's office to pick up some books on the demon clans we were dealing with. I juggled some of the old, dusty books in my good arm as we made our way into the magic shop. Chris and Tess were pouring over incantation books and taking furious notes, and they barely looked up to acknowledge us.

"I've gotta get a couple things. Wait here," Evie said as she ducked into her tattoo room.

Tess popped over without a word and slid a couple books onto the pile I was barely holding. I could feel my grip giving way and was looking for a place to dump the stack when Evelyn plucked them out of my hand and gave me a roll of tracing paper to hold instead.

"Here, carry diss," she mumbled around the cluster of markers and pencils she had shoved between her teeth.

As I followed her upstairs, we proceeded to lay claim to the kitchen table. Once Evelyn got the books set down, she took the roll of paper from me.

"Shirt off and turn around," she instructed as she proceeded to pull off a good length of paper. I was able to get it unbuttoned fine, but I still didn't have good use of my left shoulder and was having a hell of a time with the rest.

"Damn it," I complained.

She laughed and cracked a few jokes at my expense, but she did offer her assistance. I half wished I could refuse out of stubborn pride, but truthfully, I wouldn't have said no even if I didn't need it. Anything to have her in close proximity was always going to win out, no matter how much I didn't want it to. The tips of her fingers brushed my skin as she carefully slid my shirt off one arm and then the other. Folding it neatly, she hung it over the back of a chair and picked up the length of tracing paper and a marker.

"Hold still," she said as she held the paper up to my back and popped the lid off the pen.

"What are you doing back there?" I asked as I felt the felt tip of the pen move across the paper.

"Drawing a mock-up of where you already have tattoos and the general shape of your back so I know the space I have to work with for the next piece."

I nodded and closed my eyes, allowing myself to enjoy the feel of her touch for just a moment. She put the paper down on the table, and suddenly I felt her fingers on my skin, tracing the lines of the phoenix I had tattooed under my right shoulder blade.

"When did you get this?" she asked as she followed the line of the phoenix tail around my side to the top of my hip.

"Chris and I got them when we were recruited by Lebriga."

"Why?"

"'Cause chicks dig guys with tattoos."

I heard Evie huff behind me in what sounded like disgust, and she picked up the roll of paper from the table and tore off a smaller piece. The irritation on her face when she stood in front of me was clear as she placed the tracing paper over the bandage on my shoulder and began to map it out.

"What's this one for?" I asked.

"Don't worry, I'll give you something manly for the *ladies* to ogle," she shot and pressed the marker down harder than she had on my back. I turned my head to watch and saw her jaw was clenched tight. She was pissed, and for some reason that made me smile.

"Okay, I got the phoenix as a symbol of leaving my old life and starting a fresh and new one," I admitted, almost in a whisper.

"That's a decent enough reason, I guess. Now get to work; you have a lot of studying to do," she said with a slight grin as she picked up her tracings and moved to the opposite end of the table.

While I spread the books out on the table, Evie slipped off to pilfer some more comfortable chairs since we were most likely going to be at this all day. I poured over the reference books, and she worked on my tattoo templates, drilling me with questions about the different demon clans every so often. A couple times I even thought I caught her looking at me, but she was always quick to avert her eyes and play it off. Her fingers fiddled intermittently with a length of silky hair as they wound their way up to the back of her neck and rubbed the illuminated skin. She played with her hair a lot when she thought, which was probably why she wore it pulled back most of the time, but it was nice to see this side of her — a sensitive, more feminine one.

As I picked up the next book, ready to dive into its text, I noticed that it felt different than the other ones. It was smaller, bore no title, and looked more like one of Tessa's spell books than the big tomes of information. I opened the cover and read the title page. Interesting… It was a book of charms and wishes, something I'd never seen or heard of before in my limited time with the company. I was about to put it aside, thinking it had gotten into my pile by mistake, when I noticed a ribbon marker dangling from the spine. Holding the length of satin fabric with one hand, I opened the book and saw something very familiar: the tattoo on the back of Evie's neck, the Eye of Serendipity.

"What is one of the distinct characteristics of the Dichot demon?" she asked suddenly.

"Uh, um…they, uh…" I stammered, dropping the book as my brain floundered for an answer. "Crap, what do they do…oh, they always travel in pairs, couples, male and female."

"Are you all right? Maybe we should take a break and have Isolde check you out. I'm finished with these anyway." Evie looked at me over the top of her glasses while she stood up and gathered the drawings, rolling them up together.

"Yeah, okay, right behind you," I said as she trotted past me and down the stairs.

As soon as she was safely out of sight, I picked up the small book and flipped through the pages to find the right one because, in my mini freak-out, I'd lost my place. Luckily the book seemed to open to the correct page almost immediately, and I read like a fiend:

"The Eye of Serendipity: a charm of fate; a guide; a light when the path is dark and unsure."

"Today, Daniel," Evelyn barked up the stairwell.

"Coming. Damn," I called back and quickly tucked the book under one of the others.

Down in the infirmary, I wanted to ask Isolde about the Eye, but Evie never left the room. I suppose I still could have asked, but Evie wasn't hating me at the moment—she even called me by name and not *rookie*, *newbie*, or *dumb-ass*—and I kinda wanted to keep it that way for as long as I could.

So I decided to take the book back to my room to read up on the charm when everyone else had gone to sleep, but by the time we got back upstairs, the table had been cleared for dinner and the book was gone. *Damn it.* That left Plan B, my good pal Google. But, as I'd suspected, I had no such luck searching for the Eye of Serendipity or anything like it. *Double damn.*

I had one more shot: try to corner Tess, Isolde, or even Alex alone before I had to go down into Evelyn's shop for marking. Again, nothing. Everyone seemed to be moving in groups, and I couldn't catch any one of the three of them alone. At least I was nearly healed. It was only two days after the incident with the Limaske demon, and the puncture wounds had diminished to three round, pink scars. I didn't even need a bandage on them anymore.

After sucking down a hearty breakfast, I wandered down the hall into Evie's back room. She was standing at the counter, mixing ink and preparing for the session. Her hair was braided again, but I could still see the edges of the tattoo peeking out from either side of it.

I saw the tracing paper on the chair and picked it up to take a look at what I was in for.

"These are just going to be outlines," she said. "I can go back over them later and make them into a nice, cohesive back piece with the work you already have there if you want."

Ha, IF I want? If it meant long hours in close proximity with Evelyn, I seriously wanted.

"That's cool. So, what are these anyway?"

"The one with the two birds around the compass is for protection, and the trees around the swirly triangle thing is for healing. Both of these are standard and will do wonders in a nasty fight," she explained, filling a cap full of what looked to be deep purple ink. "Have a seat."

The armrests of the tattoo chair had been taken off and pieces removed from either side of the back to make it easier for me to straddle and lean forward while she worked. After prepping the area and getting the transfers on just right, Evie began.

The needle burned, and that ink stung like a son of a bitch, more than normal. But the music that she always played and the endless grilling of my demon knowledge helped to take my mind off the pain. Kinda. Okay, not really, but it did help me keep my focus on the job and not the swirls of ink under her braid or the feeling of her hot, gloved palms splayed across my back.

The tattoos went on fairly fast, even with the breaks we both needed to take during the process. When my back was finished, she covered the fresh ink with loose bandages and prepared to start the piece on my shoulder.

I noticed as she moved in closer, practically up under my chin, that she was uncharacteristically quiet while she worked. Shouldn't she have still been drilling me about what accent to use with which dialect of this beast or that? She'd hardly stopped talking to take a breath when she had worked on my back, and there was no possible way there wasn't something else she could have been teaching me right then. That's not how she worked.

"What's this one for?" I finally asked, not able to stand the silence any longer.

"Um," she said, clearing her throat, "it's a tradition in our house to be marked after you complete your first assignment."

"That's cool." I smiled, a sense of pride welling up in me. "I almost feel like I belong here now."

"You belong here," she said so quietly I could barely hear her over the buzz of the tattoo gun in my ear, and honestly, I wasn't quite sure I was supposed to.

"It looks like Japanese, but it's hard to tell upside down," I said before the silence hanging between us got overtly awkward.

"It is. Alex asked me to pick out something appropriate. Can you read it?"

"Maybe, if I actually read Japanese. I was totally guessing," I confessed.

She finished the last line and turned off the gun. Wiping off the excess ink and blood, she then slathered a layer of Tess's ointment over the tattoo.

"It stands for courage and valor," she said as she taped down a square of gauze.

Smoothing down the last piece of tape, she finally looked up at me, her fingers still lingering on my collarbone. I could almost feel an electrical charge in the room, and I couldn't stop myself. I reached out and brushed a stray lock of hair behind her ear. For the first time, she didn't pull away.

I felt her hand reach down and her thumb move over the tail of the phoenix. It was so strange, but it almost felt like the entire tattoo came to life through her touch. She had that look in her eyes, and I could practically hear her voice in my head:

Kiss me. Kiss me. Kiss me.

I slid my thumb over the skin just under her earlobe as I leaned in. The tip of my finger reached around to the back of her neck, and I could feel the magic run up my entire arm, pulling me in.

That moment, I understood the Eye of Serendipity charm.

"A charm of fate; a guide; a light when the path is dark and unsure."

Evelyn and I were meant to be. The pull to her was something I felt down in my soul, as natural as hunting. Fated.

Her lips had barely moved against mine when a loud, obnoxious knock pounded on the backroom door so hard it rattled on the hinges.

"Yo!" Tony hollered as he flung the door open. "You two! Isolde wants to know how much longer you're gonna be? Dinner is just about ready."

Evie jumped backward. She looked panicked, and she rushed past Tony and out of the room.

Shit.

"Evie, wait!" I called and tried to go after her, but she was fast and I was encumbered by the flesh wall that was Tony. "Damn it!" I yelled when it became clear I wasn't going to catch her.

Chapter 10
EVELYN

I couldn't get out of the room fast enough. Rushing up the stairs, I blew past Isolde in the kitchen and didn't stop until I was safe in my room. I ripped my sock drawer open, reached behind it, and tore off the packet of cloaking powder I kept taped to the back of it for emergencies. Sound echoed off the bathroom walls as I performed the spell as fast as I could, before I could change my mind. I had to get out of there; I needed to think.

Taking the back stairs, I hurried to the garage and pulled my helmet out of the locker. Josie and Meg were not going to be happy I took a bike without going through them, but they'd get over it.

The cool wind whipped over my body as I passed through the gates and wound up on Mulholland as fast as I dared. I didn't go very far, just enough to catch my breath. But the strange thing was, I'd never felt so breathless.

Here I was, one hundred and thirty-five goddamn years old, I'd faced down some of the nastiest creatures ever imagined, and I was petrified to kiss a boy. How ridiculously absurd was that? As I sat on the side of the road, looking out over the city, I could feel the ink burn under my skin.

I remembered like it was yesterday the moment Tess and I had found the book of charms at the bottom of an old box. We had thumbed through the pages, and when we got to the Eye, it had practically leapt off the page at me, lighting up with a virtual rainbow of color that apparently only I could see. Tess had insisted that was a sign and marked me that very night.

To be perfectly honest, I hadn't thought the charm really worked all that well. Over the years, it had warmed or cast a dim glow at one time or another, but never anything like this — the magic in the charm was burning through to my soul, pulling me back to the house, back to Daniel.

Damn him. That moment, that fraction of a millisecond his lips had brushed against mine, I'd known I was in over my head.

When I was sure everyone would be in bed, I snuck back into the house. I saw a scarf hanging off the doorknob to my bedroom and knew Josie was in there with Tony. I contemplated crawling into bed with Tess like I usually did, but she would want to talk about what happened and I wasn't even sure myself, so I opted for the tattoo room instead.

As I curled up on the big black chair, I saw something balled up over in the corner — a shirt…Daniel's shirt. With a quick glance at the door, I leapt off the chair and snatched the tee off the floor. I promised myself I wouldn't smell it, that I was only going to use it as a makeshift pillow, but temptation proved too strong. I held up the red cotton shirt and took a good whiff before I tucked it safely under my head. It smelled like him: warmth, sweetness, and masculinity blended together in perfect proportions.

Damn, damn, damn.

"Evie…Ev, wake up."

Jolting awake, I almost fell out of the tattoo chair.

"Whoa, careful. Bad dream or something? You're all flushed and sweaty." Daniel rolled over to the side of the chair on my work stool.

"What?" I muttered groggily as I sat up. I had to blink a few times before I realized where I was and what was going on…I had been asleep, and the Daniel I'd been passionately making out with just seconds before had all been a dream — induced by the scent of his damn shirt, no doubt. "Oh, um…yeah. I mean, no, it was just…weird."

"I can live with weird," he said, propping his elbow on the padded arm of the chair and setting his chin in the palm of his hand. He grinned at me like he was in on some unspoken secret, like he knew that my pulse still raced, my lips still tingled, and I could still taste his tongue in my mouth.

"What does that mean?" I asked as I hopped out of the chair and over to the small sink at the counter, trying to put as much distance between us as I could. I splashed some cold water on my face, hoping to wash off the effects of the dream.

"Nothing. You were saying my name in your sleep, is all," he said. He turned on the stool and launched himself across the room.

"I was not!" I hollered, spinning around, water dripping off my face and soaking my shirt.

"You most certainly were," he said and plucked one of my sneakers off the floor.

"Give me my shoe."

"Just admit it, Evie, you like me."

"I can't stand you."

"That's not what your tattoo says." He spun on the stool, swinging my sneaker around in the air by the laces before he tossed it onto the chair.

"What? I-I…"

"Listen." He hopped off the stool and sauntered over, backing me up against the wall with his arms outstretched on either side of me, trapping me there. He leaned down until his lips were next to my ear, and I could feel his hot, moist breath on my neck. "When you're ready to finish what you tried to start last night, come and find me. I'll be around, and I'm more than ready to take this further. Ball's in your court, gorgeous."

With that, he quickly kissed the end of my nose, turned on his heel, and disappeared through the door, brushing past Tess as he strode down the hallway.

My mouth dropped open in shock. Who was *this* guy? This Daniel wasn't the cock-of-the-walk who'd come out of the Nevada desert, the one that irritated the piss out of me. He was something more. This Daniel made my skin heat, my muscles tremble, and my body snap into a state of arousal that scared me a little bit. This Daniel was undeniably hot. I felt like my bones had liquefied, and I slid down the wall, landing in a puddle on the floor.

"What in the blue hell was that all about?" Tess asked as she poked her head into the backroom.

I explained the whole thing to her, from the time Tony had interrupted my kiss with Daniel the night before to now with him ducking out of the shop and everything in between, including the dream.

"Okay, explain this to me," she said as she massaged her temples with her fingertips. "Why the hell are you sitting there on the floor instead of running after him, and, as Daniel so eloquently put it, finishing what you started last night?"

"Um…"

"Um? Um! Good Christ, woman, you are a complete social cripple, aren't you?" She grabbed me by my shoulders and steered me toward the door. "Okay, here's what you're going to do. You are going to go upstairs and at the very least take a shower because, let's face it, sister, you slept in a chair all night and quite frankly look like shit."

"Gee, thanks."

"Just keepin' it real. Now, go wash the chair stank off you, find Danny Boy, and for God's sake, get out of your own way, Evelyn."

After she had marched me upstairs and practically tossed me into the shower, I rifled through my closet and found one of the blouses that I didn't wear very often. Tess offered to let me borrow something of hers, but our styles were very different, and while I *did* want to look pretty, I still wanted to look like me. I left my hair down as well because Daniel had seemed to like it the other day. Staring at my reflection in the mirror, I felt my stomach turn over. I was really going to do this.

The house was quiet as I looked for Daniel, checking the upstairs and ground floor and stopping into the library, just in case. When I didn't find him in the training room or the weapons locker, that really only left one place: the subbasement. We had a complete firing range down there for any weapon imaginable.

I made my way down the final flight of stairs to the door of the range, and I could see Daniel through the little round window. He was wielding a compound bow, pulling back the string with his left hand, which seemed strange because he was right-handed. Opening the door as silently as I could, I stepped inside and clung to the back wall, trying to sink into the plaster and disappear. Daniel took his aim, and I watched the arrow sail through the air, hitting the target in the same space as three arrows already embedded into the bull's-eye.

"Isolde said that this is good physical therapy for my shoulder. Do you shoot?" he asked, and he pulled another arrow out of the quiver on the table next to him and nocked it against the string. His jaw clenched in discomfort as he drew and released.

"Not really," I said, nervously tucking my hair behind my ear. Why the hell hadn't I braided it?

"Come here," he said, waving me over.

I willed my legs to work properly as I made my way across the room and stood on the opposite side of the small square table. He reached over, took my hand, and tugged me in front of him.

"What's the matter, Evie? Are you afraid to be next to me, worried you won't be able to control yourself?" He gave a teasing smirk as he stepped in behind me and put the bow in my hands.

"No," I lied.

"Liar," he whispered, "but I'll let that slide. I'm not going any-where." His lips brushed against the shell of my ear as he curled my fingers around the bow. I felt him slide the arrow into my hand, and he helped me nock it. His hands never left mine, and we drew the bow and anchored it at the corner of my mouth. "Take a deep breath and let it out slowly while you take your aim and release."

His lips had fluttered along the column of my neck as he spoke, and the arrow flew to the left, missing the target completely.

"You missed, rookie." He chuckled and reached into the quiver to pull out the last arrow. Wrapping his fingers over mine, he pulled back the string. "Try it again and focus on one thing. It doesn't have to be the target, it can be anything: the feel of the bow, the tension of the string" — he leaned in closer — "the sound of my voice," he whispered, "or the pounding of your pulse." The gentle press of his lips on my neck made me catch my breath in surprise. I felt his hands skim down my body to my hips and square them.

"Why are you doing this?" I managed to squeak out in a shaky voice.

"Because I know you won't."

I don't remember how everything happened, but the bow fell from my hands and clattered to the floor as Daniel turned me in his arms. His soft palms cupped my face as he kissed me, firm and confident, our lips molding to each other's. My body snapped taut as I felt the brush of his tongue along my bottom lip, and I opened automatically. The sweet warmth of his mouth bombarded my system, and I felt my knees start to buckle. With a quick breath and a quiet groan, he pulled me closer, kissing me with newfound voraciousness, and I burned from my lips down to my toes. I felt both drunk and drugged when I finally came up for air.

"There, now was that so bad?" he asked.

"Torturous," I answered, struggling to regulate my rate of breathing. "You said you could wait."

"Yeah, I lied."

Chapter 11
Daniel

I kissed her good and sound with everything I had. My left hand slid down Evie's back, over the swell of her full backside as I pulled her closer still, my shoulder burning with pain until her ass muscle flexed in my grip and I forgot about any pain I was feeling.

"Evie," I whispered as I leaned in, dropping open-mouthed kisses along the curve of her neck, "I'm going to trace every single line of every single tattoo on your entire body."

"Is that a threat?" she challenged with a mischievous smile as I turned her around and swept her hair off the back of her neck, exposing the Eye of Serendipity. It was illuminated in a near-blinding white.

"It's a promise." I closed my eyes against the bright light of the glowing ink and pressed my lips to it. The magic jolted through my body, and my mouth tingled. I moved my hands under the hem of her blouse and across the bare skin of her quivering belly.

"Please," she breathed, reaching a hand back and curling her fingers into my hair, pulling it, urging me on.

The range door swung open and cracked against the wall next to it.

"The hunters are back; they got past the barrier," Finn rambled, out of breath.

He disappeared almost as fast as he'd barged in, but by then Evelyn had stiffened in my arms, and I could feel the air around us had changed from open and sensual to all business. I let go of her, and she darted for the door like an escaping animal. I chased after her, caught her in the stairwell, and pinned her to the wall.

"What the hell are you doing? We have to go."

"I know, I just want you to know that this isn't done." I nodded my head to indicate the two of us. She looked at me strangely, like she didn't understand what I was talking about. I leaned in close and traced the tip of my nose along her ear. "I keep my promises," I whispered, pressing my body against hers, which trembled as she took a shaky breath and swallowed hard. Yeah, she knew what I meant now.

"Guys, come on," Finn hollered from upstairs, the cock-blocking little shit.

Evie elbowed me out of the way and ran up the stairs without another word or look in my direction. I clomped up behind her, trying to catch up, but she was too far ahead of me; I didn't reach her until she was crossing the threshold into the conference room. I grabbed her wrist, intent on finding out just what her problem was, why she always bolted at the first possible opportunity.

That's when I saw Tony, Josie, and Z.

Dear God.

Josie and Tony clung to each other as if their lives depended on it while Isolde hugged Z's head, stroking his hair like a mother would a terrified child.

"Jesus Christ," I said at the thick scent of vomit in the room. Evelyn leaned into me and clench my hand, just for a second. It felt almost like she needed reassurance of some kind; I needed it too. I slid my hand down to the small of her back, casually urging her closer, and rubbed in a tight circle. I sensed that was what she needed in that moment and prayed she wouldn't whip around and snap my wrist like a twig; you just didn't know with her. She didn't, and after a few seconds of this consolation, we made our way over to the table and took the last two empty chairs, luckily side by side.

"Now that we are all present, we should begin while everything is fresh in everyone's mind," Alex said with a nod to the current field team.

Tony made a strange face as he released Josie and reached back over the side of his chair. He pulled up a small green trashcan and proceeded to wretch into it. "Sorry," he croaked apologetically to the room, "I tried to keep it in, but when I think about what we saw…" He made that face and hugged the bucket again. Walter grabbed the vomit-filled trashcan and handed him an empty one.

Alex squeezed his eyes shut; clearly it hurt him to see his hunters in that state. You could see him will the emotion down into his gut, steeling his spine and getting back down to business—there was no time for coddling now.

Z, being the specialist when it came to demons and other netherworld scum, took point. "I've seen a lot of sick shit, but this… what this Mzetir is doing—" He paused, and I could only imagine he needed to take a moment to gather his thoughts and compose himself "—it's far worse in there than what I was led to believe by my informants." He tried to continue, but the words just wouldn't come out. Finn, his handler, stood next to him and took up where he left off.

"They've taken over the hospital in their grid, using it to run experiments. Not just forced evolution but cross-pollination."

"What the hell does that even mean?" Evie asked. She gripped the arm of the chair, her knuckles turning white as the bones strained against the flesh. I slid my hand over hers, hoping to calm her and myself. To my surprise, she turned her hand and threaded her fingers between mine.

"It means they are cross-breeding," Alex answered.

"So, they're trying to make some kind of demon hybrid?" I asked.

"They already have," Z answered.

"Oh my God," Chris said as he reached for Tess and pulled her closer.

Z curled into Isolde's protective embrace as he continued. "They're mixing within the clans, with goblins, trolls…and humans."

"How does that even work? Is something like that even possible?" I wondered aloud.

"The only thing we can come up with is that Mzetir has figured out how to isolate traits within the demon and other genomes, harvesting the strengths and discarding the weaknesses," Z explained. "Sort of like a DNA Frankenstein."

"Fortunately," Alex interjected, "from what Zachary's inside source says, there have only been a handful of successful products of his experimentation."

"Okay." Evie nodded and released my hand, switching into full hunter mode. "What kind of numbers are we talking about? Two, five, a dozen? What exactly is considered a handful?"

"We weren't able to get any more information than that. The spell around us broke while we were inside, but we saw a pair of them," Josie explained.

"The human hybrids, a male and a female. Twins," Z said coldly.

The phone in front of Alex rang, and we all stared at it. Everyone who lived in the house was in the room, so there was only one person it could be.

"Yes," Alex said once he picked up the receiver. "Yes, sir…" His eyes darted to me for a split second. "I understand. I have the element in-house…yes, it will be done right away."

After hanging up the phone, he called Evie over and whispered something to her; she nodded obediently and disappeared without a word.

"Isolde," Alex continued, "I want you to take Josephine, Anthony, and Zachary to the infirmary. I don't want any of them making another move until they've been cleared, understood?"

"Of course," she said, and she stood and followed the hunters out of the room.

"The rest of you should resume your projects posthaste. This new information, albeit limited, reiterates that we must strike sooner rather than later," Alex said.

I stood with the handlers, preparing to go back to my studies and physical therapy when he stopped me. "Daniel, I'd like a moment, please."

Closing my eyes, I sank back into my chair with a suspicious feeling that I was about to get pulled from the assignment. I was new and recently injured, and although I was healing remarkably well, it just made sense. I was a liability to the team, one they couldn't afford to have out in the field.

"Wow, that's not exactly the reaction I thought I'd see," Evie said as she walked through the door, hefting a wooden box with what looked like an elongated leather pouch on top of it.

"I haven't told him yet," Alex said before I could ask what the hell she was talking about.

She set the items on the table in front of him and stood to his right. That's when I noticed that her sword was strapped to her back. Alex pulled the large leather pouch off the top of the box and set it on the table. It made a soft clunking sound that indicated there was something heavy and metal inside. The box was long with ancient symbols carved into the old, nearly petrified wood. I recognized some of the carvings and had heard of those boxes before; there was only one thing that could be inside.

"Holy crap, are you frickin' serious?" I asked, frozen where I was, staring at the script on the box.

"Very serious," Alex answered.

"Corporate hasn't issued a Divinity blade since—" I had to stop and think before I looked up to Evie "—you."

"I know," she said as she reached back and pulled her sword free. Ancient symbols illuminated along the length of the blade as she drew the tip across her palm. The same markings appeared on her flesh, lighting up and down both of her arms.

"Daniel, you are a weapons specialist, so tell me what you know about the Divinity blade," Alex asked as he reached into the leather pouch.

"It's one of the most powerful weapons in Lebriga's catalogue, if not *the* most powerful when wielded at full strength."

"Precisely," Alex confirmed, pulling a blade out of the pouch. He tapped the tip on the table, and the ancient steel sang for him. He touched a finger to the edge, drawing blood, and the entire weapon sprang to life. The glowing script rippled down the metal and into his arms, casting a light under the sleeves of his shirt.

"Holy shit," I gasped.

"Something like that, yes." Alex smiled in evident admiration of his sword. "You know, I was almost done in by a Limaske bite myself on my first time out," he mused as he turned his blade this way and that.

"You're a hunter?"

Rolling his wrist, he twisted the blade over his head and back down again. "Indeed. Who do you suppose taught this one all she knows?" He nodded to Evelyn.

I hadn't really thought about it much, to be honest. "And who trained you?"

"Perhaps some other time," he said, shoving the ancient box forward with the tip of his sword.

"I don't understand," I said, shaking my head. "Why would corporate issue this now? Don't get me wrong; I'm grateful to be given this honor, but Evie's blade was ineffective against that evolved Limaske. What good is this going to do against some souped-up hybrid that's more than likely twice as lethal? This has got to be a mistake."

"There's no mistake. Open it."

"I can't. I haven't been at this long enough. You have to give it to Tony, Josie, or Z."

"This is not meant for them; it's meant for you."

"Why me? They've been doing this a lot longer, and besides, I'm injured. I'm not even up to the getting in the ring barehanded, let alone with a weapon like this."

"I don't know why you, Daniel. All I know is that this box has been with me for many years, as was Evelyn's box before it was issued to her. Certain things aren't for us to question, they just are. Now open it." Alex smiled and tapped the lid with the tip of his sword.

A strange feeling came over me as I stared down at the box, an odd sensation drawing me in with a sense of urgency, a pull deep in my bones. The brass hinges were polished and looked bright against the old, stained wood. I touched the carvings; the surface was sanded smooth, almost silky in texture, sending zings up through my finger tips. Laying my hands flat against the sides, I could feel the vibration of the sword inside and the magic it held, even through the wood.

"Whoa," I whispered. My heart began to beat with something I couldn't explain, a super-charged sort of excitement and energy rolling through me as I pushed open the lid.

The blade inside was magnificent, bright silver with elegant script etched from tip to hilt. The incantation continued around the handle, the metal there slightly raised like Braille.

I wanted to touch it; I wanted to pick her up so badly I could practically taste the metal in my mouth. Steeling my courage, I reached into the box and wrapped my hand around the handle. The raised metal sank into the flesh of my palm, and the Divinity's magic flowed into me, filling my senses. I could feel it course through my veins as the ancient spell burned onto my skin. It moved up my right arm, marking across my chest and down onto my left bicep, glowing brightly, opening up sections of my brain that I didn't even know I had.

"Hold her with both hands. It completes the circuit of the spell," Evie said.

I raised my left hand and wrapped it around the other side of the handle. Magic hummed through my body, and I could feel the raw power deep inside my muscles and bones. Spells, incantations, and defensive and offensive moves that I hadn't learned yet unfolded inside my head. The sword had initially seemed heavy and awkward. But now it was light as air and felt like an extension of my body, like part of it. This was the most glorious weapon I'd ever wielded, bar none.

"One blade is a powerful force to be reckoned with and, indeed, *two* virtually unstoppable. But three," Alex said, indicating the three of us, "that's the closest thing to the hand of God himself."

He twirled his sword, tossing it from one hand to the other as he turned on his heel with Evie two steps behind. I fell into step, and we stalked down the hallway. I had no clue where we were going, but I bet we looked pretty freaking cool.

We headed downstairs into the subbasement and behind the range to the morgue where Z, Finn, and Isolde performed autopsies on demons they wanted to study. Spread out on the slab was that big Limaske, sans his right claw and the left two-thirds of his head, thanks to my .45. They hadn't been able to begin the autopsy process, however, because they'd yet to find anything short of a grenade that would penetrate the creature's hide.

Alex jumped onto the table with one giant leap and straddled the demon's body. He arched his blade back and brought it down, slicing a quick Y right through the chest and down the abdomen like he was carving a Christmas turkey. He leapt off the table, tucking his body into a flip and landing back on his haunches, his blade ready to strike.

"Damn," I said. I never would have guessed in a million years that Alex had that side to him. He was a serious badass.

"Evelyn and I will work with you on how to make the best use of your blade," he said as he stood, pulled the handkerchief from his pocket, and carefully wiped the sword clean. "Once you are cleared by Isolde, that is."

He smiled to himself as he tucked the cloth into the front pocket of his trousers, and I could almost see the wheels in his mind turning. He waved us out of the morgue and onto the range floor.

"Wait here," he whispered as he silently sprinted up the stairs. He was back down in a few seconds, still wearing that very suspicious grin. "You have one hour to test your blade," he said to me as he leaned through the doorway. He looked to Evie and raised a cautious eyebrow. "Go easy on him, for God's sake. If he gets hurt, it's my ass…and yours."

Disappearing up the steps, he finally left Evie and me alone. She looked so amazing when she had that sword in her hands.

"So, your ass is pretty much in my hands. Not gonna lie, I kinda like that idea," I said as I looked her up and down.

"Your hands aren't coming anywhere near my ass." She bit her lip to keep from grinning at me and swiped her blade through the air.

"I didn't hear you complaining when we were in here earlier."

We started to circle each other. She narrowed her eyes and lunged, swinging out at me fast and sudden. My sword came up practically by itself and blocked the attack with a clang as metal connected with metal. The blades crossed over our heads and ground against each other as I took a step closer to her. My body loomed over hers, and I could feel her warm breath on my chin as she stared at my mouth, licking her lips nervously. I could sense she wanted to kiss me as much as I wanted to kiss her, but we were both too stubborn to give. The energy in the room was thick, charged with magic and whatever the hell was between us. We both stepped back and circled again, mirroring our movements. Right foot over left, eyes locked, and swords at the ready.

I charged first that time, letting my instincts guide me, but she was quick and deflected my blade with ease. Our weapons blurred through the air in a flurry of thrusts and parries as they clanged and clacked together. A few sparks shot out from between our swords when they tangled over our heads, stuck together at the hilts. We found ourselves chest to chest again. I could feel her body trembling against mine as we stared at each other.

"What are you waiting for, Ev," I panted, completely out of breath from our sparring, "an invita—"

Her sword clattered to the floor as she dug her fingers into my hair and crushed her mouth to mine.

She whipped her legs around my waist when I scooped her up and pressed her against the nearest wall, kissing her for all I was worth. I worked my hands over her backside, squeezing and releasing the heavenly flesh as our tongues wrapped around each other.

Her heels dug into my back as she whimpered into my mouth and pulled away.

"Wait," she said, "we can't do this."

CHAPTER 12
EVELYN

"What?" Daniel asked as I carefully unwound my legs from his torso and stood on my own, trapped between his hard, hot body and the cool stone of the wall. He stared down, utterly dumbfounded. "I thought—"

"I know." I smoothed away the worry lines on his face with my thumbs. His arms were still wrapped around my waist, and I could feel his fingers under my shirt, sweeping across my back. I didn't want to leave the confines of his embrace, but I had to get some distance if I was going to think clearly. Daniel had a way of clouding my mind when he was that close. I wriggled out of his arms and into the open area of the range. "We have to stop, stay focused."

"I don't know about you, but I was pretty freaking focused just a minute ago."

"You know damn well that's not what I meant," I said, pinching the bridge of my nose. "If we aren't focused and on point on this assignment, we might as well just hand Los Angeles over to Mzetir and his…whatever the hell they are. I don't want to do that, do you?"

I leaned over to pick up my blade. When I stood, I realized Daniel was right behind me. He smoothed his hands over my shoulders and nudged my braid to the side with his nose.

"Do we have to stop everything?" he teased, kissing the side of my neck.

"No," I breathed as my body sank back into his. *Lips so soft, tongue so smooth and…wait…*"Yes," I corrected, coming to my senses and squirming away from him, "we have to stop doing this." I rubbed my neck, trying to erase the delectable feeling of his lips off of me. "Focus, complete and total focus."

"God, why are you so afraid to get close to me?" He scrubbed his hands over his face, the muscles in his shoulders tense.

"I'm not afraid of you. You just…you don't understand," I said, pacing the room like a troll cornered by a pack of hunters. Truth be told, that's how I felt with him standing in front of the only exit out of the room.

"Then explain it to me. Use small words if you think you have to, but please, just talk to me."

"I'm a hunter; hunting is all I know, Daniel. Everything that I am and everything that I ever will be. I've hunted for a hundred and twelve out of the hundred and thirty-five years I've lived. But you, you come in here fresh out of the real world, and, well…I haven't been in the real world for a long time. I don't remember much of my life from before what I am now, and what few memories I do have…I don't know what's real and what I've read in my file anymore."

Daniel swept a long finger across my cheek, brushing off a tear that I hadn't even known spilled over. Up until that point in my life, I'd done a pretty good job keeping everything hidden well. How the hell had he managed to waltz in here and knock all my walls down in one fell swoop?

"I'm real, and this is real," he said as he leaned his forehead against mine. I felt his fingers reach around and trace the lines of the tattoo on the back of my neck. "Please don't ever doubt that, Evie." He leaned forward and kissed my forehead before he backed off and picked up his blade.

"Thank you."

"For what?" he asked.

"For trying to understand."

He sighed and shook his head. "I'd do anything for you. I really wish you'd get that," he said, and he turned and disappeared up the stairs.

After dinner, Alex asked me to assist Tess in the shop. We needed to beef up the potion, and having two magic specialists would certainly speed up the process. Daniel still wasn't cleared for training, and until then, he would shadow Alex and study demonology, which meant I wouldn't see him much. I thought that was a good thing. I could get my head on straight without him distracting me.

But after two days of only seeing him in passing, I was utterly miserable. I hadn't realized how much I'd grown to need him. How much it calmed me just to pass him in the hallway or in the kitchen. I was so desperate to be near him, I even stood outside the men's dorm room one night and contemplated going in.

On the third day, I took my time getting ready in the morning. Hell, I wasn't in any rush to spend another day with Tess, as much as I loved her. As I came downstairs, I found the kitchen was empty, but I could smell breakfast. I checked in the oven and found the plate Isolde had left in there to keep warm for me. I pulled a barstool up to the counter and ate in silence, wondering where everyone was but not worried enough to gobble down my meal.

After rinsing my dishes and putting them into the dishwasher, I moped down the stairs into the basement. I heard the whispers of Tess, Josie, and Meg coming from around the corner before I saw them standing at the training room observation window with their noses practically pressed to the glass.

"Look at them," Meg sighed, which was very uncharacteristic of her; she just wasn't the dreamy-sigh kind of girl.

"Holy crap, did you have any idea that's what was under the stuffy shirts and perfectly tied ties?" Tess pondered to no one in particular as she stared into the training room. "Jesus, Jo, you're hogging up the entire left side of the window."

"What the hell is going on?" I asked.

All three of them darted over and shoved me up to the glass. "That," they all said in unison.

My mouth hung open as I stared through the two-way mirror. Light swirled around the training room as Daniel, Tony, Z, and Alex sparred. Every single band of ink on every speck of visible flesh was on fire as they went round and round the room, taking swipes and stabs at each other.

"Jesus Christ," I said as I watched Daniel lunge at Tony. The muscles of his sweaty, sculpted back were downright lickable.

"I know," Josie said in wonder, "it's like a girlie wet dream in there."

"God, yes," Meg groaned as Z and Alex bounced off each other.

The image I was looked at was amazing, but more than feeling amped up and turned on, I itched to be in that room — in the thick of the fight, by Daniel's side. It was a yearning like I'd never had before.

I watched as Tony set him up for an attack, and my instinct took over. I was through the training room door and headed for Tony, intent on removing his head, before I even realized I'd moved. Alex hooked my arms around my back as I tried to pass him and held me where I was.

"Better to stumble in here and learn than out there and die. Just watch," he said as I fought against his grip.

"*Kef'oc b'crol*," Daniel murmured with a stomp of his foot, his hands flexed and extended in front of him. There was a loud crack as Tony hit his hands and flew backward into the wall.

"Nicely done," Alex commended, and he released me.

Daniel took a sweeping bow before he trotted over and helped a shaken Tony to his feet.

"Damn, Dan, that was some mad shit, man," Tony said as he stumbled for a moment, still trying to shake the cobwebs out of his head. "Good on ya." He slapped Daniel on the back, nearly knocking himself over in the process.

"Are you okay?" Daniel asked as he helped Tony steady himself. "I'm sorry; I didn't mean to hit you that hard."

"*Pffft*, it's all good, bro. I can handle it," Tony assured him, swaying on his feet.

Z scooped Tony up under the left shoulder and held onto him tightly. "I'm gonna go lay him down before he hurls on something."

"I'll help you," Alex said, taking Tony's other arm. "Daniel, you stay here and work with Evelyn."

"Yes, sir," we both said at the same time.

For whatever reason, that made Alex smile wide and proud. "Excellent," he said as he gave us a nod, then helped Z escort Tony to the infirmary for a once-over.

I stared at the floor while everyone but Daniel filed out of the training room. I know it was chicken-shit to not look at him, but I couldn't without wanting to leap on him and kiss him. The way he moved when he was fighting was decidedly feline, but not at all in a feminine way. He was raw power — sleek, confident, fluid, and sexy all at the same time — and my hormones were finally joining the party.

"That was…impressive," I said, nodding at the floor and trying to sound casual and nonchalant.

"Thanks, Alex taught me that yesterday. I guess I need to work on my control. Tony's gonna be okay, though, right?" he asked.

I finally gave in and looked up at him. He was rubbing the back of his neck and looked so worried that he might have hurt a member of the team.

"He'll be fine. I've done worse to him, trust me." That seemed to make him feel better.

"I'll bet you have. Wanna see what else I learned?" he asked with a smile.

My right eyebrow shot up. *Listen up, Ev, you need to focus*, I chided myself as I looked his sweat-covered body up and down. *Time to practice what you preach, sister.*

"Okay, show me what you got," I replied with far more innuendo than was appropriate.

"Any day of the week, baby, but we should probably stay focused on training, hmm?" His smirk spread into a full-blown, panty-melting grin.

Holy shit.

I whispered the strength spell under my breath as I grabbed him by the wrist. Leaning in with my hip, I immediately wrenched him over my shoulder before I totally caved and jumped on him right there in the training ring.

Daniel hadn't been on the ground for more than a millisecond when he popped up off of his back. He winked at me, and the next thing I knew, the room spun around me, and I was the one flat on my back with him pinning me to the mat like a bug. He held my arms at the wrist, above my head. His nose was just inches from mine, and I could feel the sweat from his chest seeping through my shirt.

"Not bad," I croaked. I tried to catch my breath, but that was very hard to do with Daniel sitting on my midsection and looking at me like I was something to eat.

"Thank you."

I thought for a moment he might try to kiss me, but to my grave disappointment, he let me up without even an inappropriate comment, damn it.

We started again, sizing each other up as we moved around the floor, each of us waiting for the other to strike at any given moment. Not being one who was overly patient, I decided to take another swipe at him.

I took a breath to begin the string of incantations I was going to use against him when he spoke: "I missed working with you the last few days."

"What?" I stopped and stared at him.

"Not just working with you, I missed *you*," he corrected, closing the distance between us. "I missed everything about you, Evie, and I'm really sorry."

"You're sorry for missing me?"

"No, I'm sorry about this," he said, and he kicked my feet out from under me, and I landed square on my back.

That sneaky little shit. Alex *had* taught him well indeed; he was using my weakness — him — against me. Two could play that game.

While he was busy gloating, I swept his legs, and he tumbled like a house of bricks. I scrambled over to claim my victory, but that was quite short-lived. We rolled and struggled for dominance, yelling, grunting, and laughing. I freely admit I allowed him to have the upper hand on more than one occasion because I liked the delicious press of his body over mine.

Like just then, lying there underneath him like that, panting and covered in perspiration, magic pulsing through our bodies. He was lingering, threading his fingers through mine, our heads pressed together.

"Evelyn," he whispered and moved in to kiss me. I felt myself melt into him as my palms moved over the phoenix on his back and his tongue slid easily into my mouth.

"Ya know, that works a lot better without clothes," Z said, leaning against the doorframe.

"We're training," Daniel said. He stood and extended a hand to me, helping me off the floor.

"Riiiight. Look, Tess has a new batch of magic juice that's ready for testing. When you two are done making out and playing grab-ass, that is." Z rolled his eyes, turned on his heel, and left.

"You ready for this, to go back out in the field?" I asked.

"Are you kidding?" Daniel laughed as he rubbed the white towel around his torso, mopping up the sweat.

"No, I'm not kidding. I don't want you going out if you aren't one hundred percent."

Daniel just grinned and shook his head at me. "You know you're adorably sexy when you're serious." He gave my backside a smack as he passed and headed for the door. "I need to hit the showers. Wanna come?" he asked, wagging his eyebrows at me.

YES!

"No," I scoffed, shoving him away from me.

"God, you're a terrible liar, Ev. You bite your lip when you do it. I'll meet you in Alex's office in twenty," he said with a wink and disappeared down the hall.

I watched Daniel's backside as he trotted up the stairs before I left the training room and made my way to Alex's office. Apparently we had been at it in the ring for longer than I'd thought, because he was back to his usual boss-man self, complete with tie and suit vest.

"So, I gather you aren't going with us this afternoon?" I asked as I plopped into one of the empty chairs on the other side of his desk, propping my feet up next to his antique ink well.

"No, not this time. This is just a test run and a test run only." He glared at the soles of my sneakers over the top of his glasses but didn't comment on my feet being so precariously close to one of his prized possessions. He didn't have to—the gnarled look he shot spoke volumes.

That was the thing with Alex and me: we'd been working together for over a hundred years. Words were almost superfluous at that point. Funny thing was, now that I thought about it, it was the same with Daniel, practically from day one. I slung my feet off the desktop like a good girl, but not without sighing like an annoyed teenager first.

Daniel leapt over the back of the empty chair next to me and dropped into the seat as he practically ran into the room. His hair was still soaking wet, making a ring on the back of his T-shirt collar as water dripped down his neck.

"Did I miss anything?" he asked excitedly.

"I was just telling Evelyn that this exercise is for test purposes only. I don't want anyone to get any bright ideas out there today." Alex pointedly looked at me over the rim of his glasses. "The blades will stay here, and you will both be issued a small revolver for emergencies. Let me reiterate that this is not a hunt—fact-finding only, get in and get out. Understood?"

"Yes, sir," we both said as we stood to take our leave.

We headed to the shop, taking one detour to the infirmary to check on Tony. He was doing fine, just like I'd said, and rightly pissed that he was missing out on the field trip with us. Tony did always like to be in on all the action he could get his hands on.

When we got to the shop, Tess schooled Daniel on the new batch of potion we'd concocted. Basically it was the same mix that the others had used before, just a lot more potent.

"There are also some elements in the base that mimic demon essence. We chose the one closest to Dichot because you'll be traveling together," Tess explained. "The idea is to blend in versus just masking the hunter scent. Z said the demons would be more interested in a pair of fresh humans and more likely to start poking around you guys than two of their own. Unfortunately, because we added the demon element, we had to eliminate the telepathic component; it would just be too much for your systems to juggle in one shot."

Chris breezed through the door with a pair of snub-nosed .357 Magnums, each in its own shoulder holster dangling from each hand. "These will get you two out of a jam if need be, but if you're made, you get the hell out of there but quick."

We strapped on our meager weapons and each took a cup of the frothy liquid from Tess.

"It kind of looks like beer," Daniel said, poking at the foam with his finger as I swilled down my cup full of brew.

"Oh, sweet Jesus, it sure as shit doesn't taste like it," I coughed out. Not that I was a big beer fan to begin with, but that could easily have made beer taste good.

Daniel swallowed his mouthful like a trooper, with a gag and a shudder but not a single word about the fact that it tasted like a cup of two-week-old fizzy manure water.

Down in the garage, we mounted a set of Suzuki Hayabusa's, one of the fastest street-legal motorcycles in the world.

"You break one of my babies, and I'll break all of your limbs, *capisce?*" Jo said as she handed us each a helmet.

Sitting side by side on the bikes, we watched the garage door roll up.

"Would she really break our arms and legs?" he asked over our helmets' two-way-radio.

"If we're lucky, that's all she'll do before she turns us over to Meg."

I winked before I lowered my visor and sped out of the garage.

CHAPTER 13
DANIEL

I followed Evie down the highway, watching her braid whip around as we rode toward one of the areas where we could slip into demon territory relatively unnoticed.

After parking the bikes in a non-descript drug store parking lot, we continued on foot. We ducked across the street and made our way through a car lot, moving closer to the containment field. My bones vibrated under my skin, and I could feel my stomach twisting and knotting.

"Do you feel that?" she asked.

"Yeah, we're close," I answered with a nod.

We stopped a few feet from the outer layer of the bubble where the air was distorted and swirled with the sheer amount of evil trapped on the other side. I wanted to throw up.

"Ready?" she asked, giving my hand a reassuring squeeze as we stood on the sidewalk under the shade of an office building just outside the field.

"Kiss me," I blurted.

"What?"

"I need something to ground me before I go in there, something I can hold onto, otherwise I'm going to lose my magic hold," I rambled desperately, and it was the God's honest truth.

"I really don't think—"

"Besides, we're supposed to be passing ourselves off as Dichots. We should carry each other's scent, right?"

Evie cocked an eyebrow at me, tapping the toe of her boot against the concrete and chewing the inside of her cheek as she contemplated. It was true: a pair of Dichot demons would be riddled with each other's scent if they were traveling together. Glancing around the street for a moment, she grabbed the back of my neck and hauled herself up to my mouth.

The press of her lips felt urgent, almost stiff for a second, then her fingers suddenly curled into my hair, her body molded to mine, and the taste of her minty wet tongue filled my mouth. One of her hands slid down my back and gripped the hell out of my butt cheek, urging me closer as she kissed me from every possible angle. She then pulled back slowly and rested her forehead on my chin, one hand clutching a fistful of my hair and the other a hearty chunk of my ass.

"Just in case I never get a chance to do that again," she said, then leaned forward and pressed her lips to my throat. "Or that."

"Let's do this thing," I said, still feeling the imprint of her fingers on my flesh.

Evie walked confidently down the sidewalk two strides ahead of me. As much as I wanted to be the man and enter before her, making sure the coast was clear and all that good mess, it wasn't going to happen. First and foremost, Ev didn't roll like that—not to mention, in the Dichot clan, the females took the lead and we had to play the part, which meant she went in first. We both took a deep breath and passed through the field without any hesitation. No one gave us a second glance as we strode toward Hollywood Boulevard, where Mzetir's headquarters were rumored to be. The air in there was thick and tasted stale and slightly bitter.

Evie reached up and touched the side of her sunglasses, turning on the camera in the frame—one of Walter and Tony's gadgets. These weren't some cheesy, 1.2 megapixel nanny cam in those frames; hell no, these bad boys took not one but *two* high resolution, 14.1 megapixel images through the lenses and transferred them into the mock iPod Evie had in her front pocket. I adjusted the earbud in my ear and activated the audio recorder I carried. Once we got back to the lab, the guys would dissect the sounds and isolate voices, so hopefully I picked up something useful.

There was a troll across the street looking at us, watching the way we moved and our body language toward each other. Evelyn must have noticed it as well because she reached back, grabbed my belt buckle, and pulled me a step closer, a possessive gesture that warned any observers I was her property. This seemed to satisfy the nosey, gelatinous creature because it stopped watching us.

Moving east, we walked about a city block from the W Hotel. I knew it was just perception, an optical illusion, but the plaster and brick beast with hundreds of hungry glass eyeballs and obnoxious red signs appeared to grow and pulse with life as we got closer. It was only twelve stories tall, but in close proximity, the energy it emitted was immense, giving it the feel of something much larger, dark, and evil.

As we crossed the last street, Evie stopped and turned to me, wrapping her arms around my waist and pulling me close as she nuzzled the crook of my neck.

"Coming up behind me is a man talking on his phone," she whispered. "He's going into the hotel, and I need you to bump into him with this shoulder." Her hand moved up and pressed against my right shoulder. "Make sure the powder on your jacket transfers onto him."

"How do you know that's where he's—"

"Just go, and don't apologize," she said, giving me a shove toward the man who wore a gray suit and was chattering away on his phone like he was the only person in the world.

"Email me the details. I'm going up to my room right now, and I'll look over the entire proposal and get back to you," he yakked.

I shouldn't have been surprised that she was right about this guy going into the W. Evie had a sixth sense about that kind of thing. Getting into character, I jammed my hands into my front pockets, ducked my head and plodded in his direction.

"*Oof!*" the man said when he bounced off my right shoulder. There was a slight shimmer on his left suit arm where we'd connected. "Watch where you're going, asshole," he snapped. "Stupid emo-slacker-whatever kids pay no attention…Hey, sweetheart," he leered at Evelyn as she sashayed past. Damn, she could work her walk when she wanted to.

"Hey, yourself," she said with a flirty wave and a wink.

"Don't be a stranger, honey. I'll be in the Living Room later tonight. I'll buy you a drink or three, huh?"

What a tool. He trotted up the red-carpeted stairs and through the big glass sliding doors. He wasn't inside for two seconds when he sailed back through the door, landing flat on his back in the middle of the sidewalk, followed by two of the biggest trolls I'd ever seen in full human regalia. They beat the ever-loving crap out of that poor guy before he could even try to convince them he was a guest at the hotel.

"Shit, that's what I was afraid of," Evie said as she rifled around inside her jacket and pulled out a flask.

"What? Jesus, Ev, you gotta talk to me and tell me what's going on."

"Tess and I suspected that the inside of the hotel was rigged with some type of alarm system that could detect our kind if we happened to get past their initial force field," she explained.

"And if there was anything to set it off, that powder I transferred to him was going to do it."

"Exactly."

"So what's that stuff?" I asked, nodding to the leather-covered flask in her hand.

"Hopefully this will get me inside."

"Us," I corrected.

"This isn't up for discussion," she said, unscrewing the top.

"Neither is you going in there alone, and you better hurry up because people are starting to look." I glanced around. She stared up at me, clenching her teeth and shaking her head. Pig-headed woman, I swear to God.

"Fine, but if we get caught and killed, I'm going to kick your ass."

She turned her head and drained the flask. Then, gripping the neck of my shirt, she kissed me hard, leaving half of the fluid from the flask in my mouth. It tasted gross, just like the other nasty shit Tess had made us drink, but this was a helluva lot better way to drink it down.

"Act natural and be ready to haul ass," she said, and she wrapped her hand around my waist and hooked her thumb into my belt loop.

"Do you have a plan?" I slung my arm over her shoulders, and she started doing that sashay walk again.

"Yep…the plan is to not get caught."

"Good plan," I said while we walked up the red carpet and the doors whooshed open.

She giggled in response, but it was fake and forced, a show. I could feel the muscles in her shoulders tensing and her .357 Magnum poking me in the ribs. We stepped through the threshold, and all the employees looked up.

Shit.

Luckily, they didn't give us a second glance and went on about their business as if we were regular hotel visitors. We rounded the corner, and sitting in the middle of a big round white couch on top of a pile of pillows was the most disgusting…*thing* I'd ever seen in my life. It was just lounging there out in the open, stretching its nearly human body across the obnoxious furniture. Its fingers were freakishly long and appeared to have an extra knuckle in them.

"What the fu—" I started to say before Evelyn cut me off with an elbow to the ribs and nodded to the sleek black couches in the lobby.

The thing slid off the pillows and stood, moving in a strange clipped, awkward, and downright macabre gait. Its skin slid over its bones like a weird milky gray film that looked tissue-paper thin, but I suspected it was anything but. The most disturbing part was that it wasn't even trying to disguise itself.

"Izutan, Ozael," it hissed in a somewhat female-ish voice to the two big trolls that had just re-entered from outside, "Father wants to know if you've taken care of the situation?" It—she?—sidled up to a second creature that was built very similar to her but taller and with a more masculine look about him.

These must be those creepy-ass twins Tony, Josie, and Z saw. No wonder Tony had been horking in the trashcan; those things were beyond gross-looking.

"Yes, mistress, the matter was handled," the largest one said with a bow.

The male and female stood side by side and took each other's hand, fingers interlocked, with their other hands outstretched, palms up to the ceiling. Their eyes closed, the eyeballs visibly vibrating beneath the lids.

"Very good. Father is pleased," they said in unison.

Suddenly a dozen goblins tromped through the sliding doors, carrying the body of the cell-phone guy over their heads like a trophy. His mouth was splayed open and his eyes were flat and empty.

Jesus Christ. He was dead. And I had killed him.

"Shame," the male said with a *tsk*, twisting his head unnaturally to look at the body.

"Indeed, he served Father well," agreed the female.

I felt the bile rise up in the back of my throat, but I muscled it back down. Even though that dude clearly wasn't the most moral person on the planet—aligning himself with demons and all—I was still responsible for his death.

"To the kitchen?" The male rolled his head to his sister.

The she-beast scanned the body for a moment, snatching the dead man's hand and snapping a finger clean off. She inspected the disembodied digit and clamped her teeth around its bloody end. With an audible crunch, she bit right through the bone and flesh, extracting what was left with a sickening slurp. She chewed for a few seconds and appeared to push the partially masticated finger around in her mouth with her tongue as if she were considering a fine wine.

"And so you will serve Father one last time," she cooed as she knelt down to the body and stroked her spindly fingers over his hair. "Prepare him well," she said to one of the goblins as she stood; she flipped the remainder of the finger to it, and the diminutive creature snatched it out of the air like a Chihuahua.

Evelyn was curled up against me on the black leather couch, casually tracing the design on my T-shirt with her finger as she watched the scene play out in front of us through the lenses of her photographic sunglasses. I kept my arm wrapped around her waist, rubbing up and down her back and occasionally palming her butt cheek. To everyone in the place, we appeared to be just an amorous couple and completely on par with the breed of demon we were passing for at the moment.

The cell phones in our pockets vibrated simultaneously, the signal that our time was up and we needed to boogie. We casually got up off the sofa and wandered around the lounge area, gradually making our way to the door and slipping out with a family of demons I'd never seen before. As we strolled north on Vine, Evie tucked her head under my arm until we turned down an alley between two tall buildings. Once we were obscured from view, she doubled over, clenching her stomach.

"Jesus, are you okay?" I asked before I felt the sharp jab in my own gut. "Shit!"

"The spell is wearing off. We need to get out of here, fast," she grunted.

Stumbling through back alleys, we managed to make it back to the barrier without being noticed. Thank God, because by that time I was feeling better and suspected we were basically out there naked with no magic cloaking us whatsoever.

"Damn," Evie said as she felt along the interior of the force field. She reached into her jacket pocket and pulled out an envelope. "We're going to have to run like hell because this is not going to be subtle. Step back."

We took a good five steps backward before she tossed the envelope at the invisible wall. There was a poof of green smoke and what sounded like sheets of metal ripping apart. The barrier split and retracted like it was a living thing shrinking back in pain. Grabbing my lapels, Evie tossed me through the opening and dove through after me before the hole could close. I heard the rumble of creatures in the distance getting closer by the second as we ran down the street and into the drugstore parking lot where we'd left the bikes. We slapped on our helmets and screeched out of the lot.

Neither one of us said anything as we hit the freeway, swerving in-between cars and trucks at breakneck speed. We hit the mansion's driveway in just under ten minutes, the fastest time from downtown to home base I'd ever experienced since I'd been there. As I pulled the bike into its designated slot, the weight of what we'd just witnessed closed in on me, and I started freaking out. I was responsible for killing someone, a human being.

I clawed at my helmet and couldn't seem to get it off fast enough. Evelyn was immediately at my side, pulling off my jacket and shoulder holster and speaking calmly.

"Daniel, calm down. Breathe and calm down."

"That guy, he was human…I killed him. We aren't supposed to put humans in any harm. I killed an innocent." My voice sounded shaky and echoed like a tin can inside my own head.

"First of all, you did not kill him, the trolls did that. And second, yes, he was human, but he was far from innocent. He worked with demons by choice; he gave up his innocence and his soul a long time ago. Besides, you didn't put him in harm's way, I did." She gripped my face and forced me to look at her. "We have to debrief with Alex, so you have got to pull yourself together, okay?"

Her eyes were so warm I instantly felt more at ease. She took a couple of slow, deep breaths with me, and I nodded, indicating I was ready to go.

We stopped at the lab first and handed our gadgets over to Tony and Walter so they could sift through what we'd captured in photos and sound. Once in the office with Alex, the debriefing took well over an hour. My head pounded, and I felt like I wanted to throw up as we detailed everything we'd witnessed inside the hotel lobby.

I truly thought I'd had a good bead on weird shit, but after what I'd seen today, my limited experience to date didn't even make a blip on the weird-shit radar. No wonder Evie was the way she was. She didn't have a choice; it was for survival.

I lay in my bunk that night and tried to sleep, but that guy's face kept flashing in my head, his vacant, dead eyes staring at me accusingly. Even though Alex had assured me that what I felt was normal, that they'd all been there, and that guy had been a serious sleaze, I still felt semi-responsible for his death. Turning over, I closed my eyes again. If I couldn't sleep, at least I could try to rest.

The door opened and closed. I assumed Z or Tony was finally calling it a night until I got that strange feeling that someone was watching me. I rolled over to see who was playing creeper, and a pair of Hello Kitty lounge pants stared back at me in the dark.

"Evie?" I asked, sitting up on my elbow and rubbing my eyes to make sure I hadn't in fact fallen asleep and was dreaming.

"Shhh," she hissed, glancing over her shoulder where the two beds across the room were as she sank down to the floor next to my bed. "I just wanted to make sure you were holding up okay after today. Go back to sleep," she whispered.

"I wasn't asleep, and we don't have to whisper. Tony and Z are still downstairs working." I rolled over onto my stomach and lay on my pillow, eyeball to eyeball with her.

"Oh." She sat back away from me a bit and fidgeted with the bottom of her T-shirt, looking a little uncomfortable with that information. "So...can't sleep?" she asked, hugging her knees up under her chin. "That's pretty normal."

I had to laugh. "You guys keep telling me that, but I'm still waiting for the 'normal' to kick in." I did feel a little better with the knowledge that she was worried about me, though.

"It will. Well, normal for us, anyway," she said. "Try to get some sleep. I know it's hard after today, but you need rest." She stood up from the floor and dusted off her backside as she turned to leave.

"Wait," I said, sitting up fully. "Can you just...stay, for a little bit, please?"

She chewed the inside of her cheek and twirled an errant chunk of hair through her fingers. "Just a little while. I have to get some sleep too, ya know," she said as she started to sit back down on the floor.

"No, not down there...here." I patted next to me on the bed, and she narrowed her eyes.

"I'm not sleeping with you," she said, crossing her arms over her chest and tapping a Happy Bunny slipper at me.

"That's not what I meant." *Okay, maybe I did mean it a little bit,* I thought as I went over how to explain it without sounding like a gross perv. "I just...Don't you ever just want to be normal, like normal-normal for two minutes?"

"What *exactly* do you want, Daniel?" she asked, seeming to drop her defenses as she dropped her arms.

"I just want to lay here with you. That's it. No funny business, no ulterior motives. I just *need* two minutes of normal."

Ev tucked the stray bit of hair behind her ear as she rocked back and forth, shifting the weight on her feet, her teeth working like hell over her lip.

"Two minutes?"

"That's all. Two minutes, and I promise I'll keep all of my parts to myself."

She tentatively slid her slippers off and climbed up onto the bed, crossing her legs and sitting a good three feet from me.

"Okay, two minutes," she said, looking everywhere in the room but me.

"Lay down, Ev. I'm not going to bite." I scooted down and patted the other side of my pillow and pulled the blanket back.

Moving slowly like a skittish animal, Evelyn crept across the bed, turned around with her back to me and lay down. I pulled the blanket up over us and inched as closely as I dared. Her body was stiff as a board as I wrapped my arm around her and settled in, nuzzling the back of her neck.

"Hmm," I hummed, sighing quietly as I felt her relax just a touch.

Two minutes passed into five, and we fell into a natural pattern of parallel breathing, in and out, slow and measured, until her body all but molded against mine and her foot twitched against my leg. I peeked over her shoulder, saw her eyes were closed, and heard a little snore as she took her next breath.

After about an hour, she mumbled something unintelligible in her sleep and rolled over and snuggled up into my chest, falling back to sleep. I probably should have woken her, and I was probably going to pay for this in the morning, but all I did was close my eyes, hold her close, and enjoy that moment of normalcy.

CHAPTER 14
EVELYN

"Evie…Ev…you're snoring."

"Goddamn it, Tony, I'm trying to sleep, you asshole. Now get the hell out of my room," I grumbled, yanking the pillow out from under my head and lobbing it across the room to where the sound of his voice had come from. It sailed back almost immediately and walloped me in the face.

"Newsflash, Mary Sunshine: you're in my room," he said as he walked out and pulled the door closed behind him.

"What?" Bolting up in bed, my hand landed right on Daniel's morning salute. "GAH! Sorry!" I howled, tumbled out of the bed, and hit the floor with a resounding thud.

"Shit, are you okay?" he asked, hanging over the side of the mattress.

"Yeah, but you said two minutes!" I plucked a Happy Bunny slipper out of my ass crack and launched it at Daniel's head.

"Hey, *you* fell asleep," he said as he deflected the footwear. "What was I supposed to do?"

"Uh, wake me up?"

"Hmm, wake you up, send you back to your room, and sleep alone if I could sleep at all," he said, raising one hand slightly. "Or, let you be and get to sleep with a beautiful woman pressed up against me." He raised the other hand and pretended to weigh the options.

Initially I was pissed, but how could I stay that way when he said things like that?

"All right, since you put it that way, I'll let you slide this time." I sat on the end of the bed. "So, how are you doing today?"

"Are you asking as my trainer or as Evelyn?"

"I don't understand."

"As my trainer, you're asking because it's your responsibility. If you're asking as Evelyn, it's because you really want to know."

I thought about it for a second. I really wanted to know because we *did* need to get back to training and back out into the field as soon as possible. But I also wanted to know because he meant something to me, something more than just a partner, and I wasn't quite sure how I felt about that.

"Um, both?" I said.

"I can work with both." His magnificent mouth curled into the lopsided grin that a couple of weeks ago had made me want to vomit but now made me want to grab him and suck his face off. He scooted forward until our knees overlapped, and he brushed my discombobulated braid off my shoulder. His hand slid down my back and his long, nimble fingers teased up under the hem of my shirt, touching the bare skin as he leaned in.

I couldn't breathe; I even couldn't move.

"You know, we're all alone in here," he whispered, his thumb moving over the small of my back and into the dip just above the waistband of my lounge pants.

"W-We need to focus," I stuttered as I watched him nod in agreement and continue to inch closer to my neck with his lips.

"I'm focused, very focused…on this particular spot. You know, on my first day I saw a hint of a tattoo, and I've been dying to know what it is." He swirled his middle finger over the sensitive skin of my lower back. His breath was hot on my neck as he spoke, and I had a hard time keeping my wits about me.

"I should go," I said, maneuvering myself out of his arms. "Alex is going to want to go over all the data we gathered. We should shower, and—"

"Your shower or mine?" he asked and practically leapt out of the bed. His sweatpants were hanging so dangerously low around his hips that one wrong—*or exquisitely right*—move and little Dan and the boys would be free and loose.

"Mine…I mean yours…I mean, I'm going to mine and you're staying here. I gotta go."

He stood and leaned against the wall, laughing at me as I fumbled my words like a complete idiot. I grabbed my slippers off the floor and hurried out of the room before he could say anything else.

"Enjoy your shower," he called after me while I slammed the door shut.

I quickly ran to my room, took an extremely cold shower, and snuck down into the shop, doing my best to avoid contact with Daniel. Tess was inside, looking very much like a witch cooking up some kind of brew in her cauldron and wearing that goofy pointed hat she insisted on wearing every Halloween.

"Someone didn't sleep in her bed last night," she said as she stirred the contents of her big black pot, crouching over it and releasing an annoying cackle.

"Rein it in, Witchie-poo. Nothing happened."

She tossed me a bottle of herbs, which I caught and set on the shelf in its proper spot.

"Evelyn, Evelyn, Evelyn, I honestly don't know why you just don't give in already. You know you want to, you know *he* wants to, and trust me it would be so much easier for everyone in the entire house if you two—"

"I don't *know* that he wants to. He's obviously alluded to it, but he's technically never come out and said it. And until you hear the words, there's always that the possibility it's a misunderstanding."

"Please. He almost died for you, for crying out loud."

"He's my partner, that's what partners do."

"That's a load of bullshit and you know it," she chided, grabbing the shaker next to the pot and adding a few sprinkles of green powder to her concoction. "That man loves you, and don't even try to tell me that you don't love him, otherwise you wouldn't have given more than three shits about how he was feeling last night." She walked over and leaned against the counter next to me and sighed. "I know there's got to be some convoluted reason why you're withholding your goods, so let's just put it out there on the table, okay?"

"It's not as easy as having a quick screw against the wall in the range, Tess," I said thoughtfully as I hopped up onto the counter and folded my legs underneath me. I wanted to choose my words carefully, get my point across. I tucked my hair behind my ear and twisted my fingers together while I thought. "If that's all this was, that would be fine. Hell, if that's all this was, I would have done that by now. But this is…more. I'm not interested in a means to an end or a release of pent-up sexual tension, not with him. He makes me feel like I'm more than just a hunter or a piece of ass. He makes me feel something that I haven't felt in…well, I don't know if I've ever felt this way, to be honest."

"What way?"

"Normal."

"Excuse me, ladies," Chris said, tapping on the doorframe and poking his head in. "I'm sorry to interrupt, but Tony and Walter have finished processing the pictures and sound bites from yesterday." He slapped the door and winked at Tess before he left.

"I don't know, maybe I'm over-thinking it," I said. "Maybe I do need to just get him out of my system so I can go back to being my brand of normal." I hopped off the counter with a shrug.

"No, Ev, don't do that. You don't see how much he's changed you already, do you?"

"How do you mean?"

"Evie, I've known you for over a hundred years, and it's not like I didn't love you just the way you were before, but you were…broken. You kept yourself so closed off from the world, kept even Alex, Isolde, and me at arm's length. But over the last couple weeks since Daniel's been here, you've let us in a little bit. Like this, right now — we never would have been able to have this conversation before. And don't even get me started on the way you guys are together, especially out on assignment. The way you work with each other, it's nothing short of magical. He completes you, Ev." Tess sighed and smiled wide as she took my hands in hers. I opened my mouth to talk, but she shook her head at me. "Don't say anything right now, just ruminate and absorb what you heard, okay?"

"Okay, I can do that."

"Good. Now come on, we'd better get our asses next door," she said as she reached over and turned off the burner underneath the big black cauldron.

We walked down the hall and into the lab where one wall was entirely covered with a giant monitor containing cropped and enhanced images from the previous day's assignment. There was some nasty-looking shit too, things that I hadn't seen when I was there, hiding in the background of the corrupt display that was the human-demon hybrid twins. I could see Daniel's eyes dart from picture to picture, absorbing and memorizing every single pixel of information like he was a human hard drive. He was so focused that when I stood next to him, I was sure he didn't even notice I was there. I was wrong.

"Do you even remember seeing half this shit?" he asked.

"No, it didn't seem like anything out of the ordinary, other than the Wonder Twins."

"Why is that? It's so obvious in the pictures, I can't believe we spaced all of that out," he wondered.

"Neither can I." It wasn't like either one of us, or any hunter for that matter, to miss something so blatant.

"It's a trick," Josie said as she walked into the room, shoving one of the bouncer trolls in ahead of her. "Start talking, dickhead."

"Fuck you," the creature spat. Z walked in behind Josie and thumped the beast in the back of the head.

"Mind your manners, asshole. You're in a room with the best hunters in existence, and you need to show some respect or I'll let them take your goddamned head off."

The troll hissed in response and shrank back away from Z. I saw Daniel's face twitch a split second before he sprang across the room and grabbed the troll by the throat. The creature sputtered and coughed as Daniel unleashed a series of spells that was far beyond his years; he shouldn't have even known what those spells were or what they could do yet, but he delivered them with such purpose and certainty—clearly the result of uniting with his Divinity blade.

I remembered the way that felt, the raw power and knowledge flooding every cell of my body, and as much as I hated to admit it, he was handling it a hell of a lot better than I had.

"Explain," Daniel growled in a tone I'd never heard from him.

He was downright menacing as he swung the beast around and slammed his face into the wall next to the giant screen so hard I could feel the floor under my feet rumble with the force. He pressed his forearm into the creature's throat while his entire body vibrated with rage.

"I said explain!"

The troll's mouth was moving, but the only sounds coming out were gags and gasps.

"Um, Dan, man, not to diss your interrogation techniques or anything, but you might want to ease up on his larynx, ya know, just a skosh, so he can answer you," Tony said calmly, placing a hand on Daniel's shoulder.

Daniel's chest heaved, his nostrils flared, and his jaw clenched so tightly the muscles in his face quivered as he stared down at the slowly asphyxiating troll. After about ten solid seconds, he backed off, but only slightly.

"The lobby is spelled to mask our presence, but the charm is only effective live—not against recorded images—to keep guests calm as it's happening. If anyone knew…if they saw…" the black-tongued creature choked out.

"If they knew what, exactly? As *what* is happening?" Alex asked as he studied the photos carefully.

"The abominations happening in there that go against even *our* standards." The troll laughed, like he knew something we didn't; it was a low and evil kind of sound that made my skin crawl. Daniel leaned in, baring his teeth as he whispered something venomous to the troll that I couldn't hear, his fingers pressing into the meaty flesh of the beast's throat and making his eyeballs bulge out.

"I'd cough up whatever information you have," Tony stated as he casually strolled back and forth, "'cause I have a feeling you're working my man Danny Boy's last nerve here, and I don't know if I could stop him from ripping your throat clean out."

"Daniel," Alex said in a tone I'd heard a million times over in my years—an order to back off immediately, a warning.

Daniel released the sputtering troll with a volatile growl and took a step back as the beast crumpled to the ground in front of him. That was quite impressive, as it wasn't easy even for me to disengage on command like that, let alone a rookie.

"Look at the human guests. What do you see?" the troll managed to ask when he caught his breath. We all stared at the screen, washing over images of the demon-breed mash-ups, and one thing became apparent.

"They're all female," I said, mentally counting at least twenty women in the lobby.

The troll laughed again, that maniacal bloodcurdling sound that itched at my insides, raising the hunter instinct in my bones. Like a tidal wave of muscle and rage, every hunter in the room surged toward the creature as it cringed on the floor, huddling against the wall.

"Stop! Christopher, Finneus, take this…*unholy being* to a cell until I talk to corporate," Alex said through clenched teeth. He gripped the back of the chair in front of him, clearly the only thing keeping him from joining the rest of the hunters.

The two men grabbed the troll and hauled him down the stairs to the subbasement, where we kept a small cell behind the morgue. In all honesty, I could have probably counted on one hand the amount of times it had ever been utilized; we weren't exactly in the practice of bringing things home…alive.

Looking at the women in the photos, Isolde said, "These girls all appear to be of prime breeding age. Mzetir is collecting human broodmares."

"I think I'm going to be sick," Walter mumbled; he clamped his hand over his mouth and ran out of the room.

"We have to stop Mzetir," Alex said and headed to his office. I assumed he was about to make an emergency phone call overseas for immediate orders.

I looked over at Daniel. He was pacing wildly and looked as if his skin was the only thing keeping him together at the moment. Odds were that was probably how he felt too; we all did, all keyed up with hunter energy and no release for it. Okay, that wasn't entirely true—there *were* releases.

"I'm going for a run," Z said as he lumbered out the door.

"Yeah, me too," Tony echoed, nodding to Josie, and I knew damn well the two of them would wind up naked in our room or his or, God forbid, in the garage.

A good fifteen seconds after Tony left, Jo said, "Look, we're all grown. I'm not even going to pretend I'm going for a run or some shit, so do me a favor and steer clear of the attic."

Daniel's breathing picked up as he yanked on his hair and grit his teeth in frustration. If he didn't get a hold on himself soon, he was going to wind up putting his fist through the wall or into one of Tony's precious giant screens.

"You need to help him," Isolde whispered to me as she pulled me aside and shooed Tess and Meg out of the room while Chris tried to talk to Daniel down.

"Isn't that his handler's job?" I asked, nodding to Chris.

"Generally, but he needs *you* to talk him through this, another hunter. He needs someone who has experienced what he's feeling. He is very volatile at the moment, and Chris could get hurt unintentionally," she explained with that innate sense of what someone needed that made her such an amazing healer. She whispered to Chris and gently tugged him out of the room as I walked up next to Daniel.

"Hey," I said, laying a hand on his shoulder. He jerked away from me.

"I'm sorry, it's just…I can't…my skin…ugh, my head…how do I make it stop?" he asked through clenched teeth, pressing the heels of his hands against his brow and squeezing his eyes shut. The easiest answer was to take him downstairs and let him remove that bastard of a troll's head, but that wasn't an option at the moment; we needed him for information.

"Z runs to release the pressure," I suggested, but Daniel shook his head at me.

"I hate running."

"Josie and Tony, they um…do what they do." I swallowed hard, knowing they were going at it like wild monkeys in the attic that very moment.

"No way," Daniel scoffed, shaking his head even harder. "Not that I wouldn't give my left friggin' nut to press your ass up against that wall and take the hell out of you right now, but that's all it would be—just taking, hard and rough," he said gruffly. His eyes rolled up and down my body, and he walked toward me, pinning me against the very wall in question. My breath caught in the back of my throat, and every nerve ending zinged from the top of my head to the tip of my toes.

"That wouldn't be so bad," I said breathlessly.

"I can't do that, not the first time," he whispered, a smile finally cracking the serious face he'd been wearing all afternoon. He winked, and that's when I knew Daniel was returning from the dark place no hunter ever wants to be.

My Daniel.

I felt the warm ink in the Eye of Serendipity on the back of my neck spread through my body, and I smiled. In the midst of all that insanity, I seemed to have come to terms with my feelings toward Daniel and finally understood the weight of what we were together. Tess was right: he did complete me. He filled a hole in my soul that nothing had ever seemed to come close to touching.

"First time? So you think there will be more than one?" I teased, feeling confident and comfortable being that close to him.

"I can guarantee it." He picked up each of my arms and wrapped them around his neck.

"Are you feeling better now?" I asked as I ran the tip of my finger through the back of his hair.

"Almost," he said, and he leaned forward and softly pressed his lips to mine. He hummed as he kissed me again, lingering longer, brushing his tongue along my bottom lip. "Wait, you aren't going to suddenly punch me in the throat or knee me in the junk are you?" he asked.

"Not today." I laughed as I rose up on my toes and kissed the sculpted curve of his jaw line.

"Are you feeling okay? You must have hit your head when you rolled out of my bed this morning." He laid a hand on my forehead.

"Shut up and enjoy this moment, you ass."

"Yeah, boss," he said with a grin.

He nipped along my neck, and I giggled as his fingers tickled up my sides. "God, you're such a dork."

"*Pffft*, c'mon, you know you love me."

"I know I do," I whispered.

"What did you just say?" He suddenly stopped and looked down at me, his eyes searching mine.

What *was* I saying? What if that hadn't been what he meant? What if he *didn't* feel the same? What if it was too soon to say it out loud? What if—

I stopped myself mid-ridiculous-train-of-thought and closed my eyes. I pushed all of the silly what-ifs aside and let myself really feel something for the first time in over one hundred years.

"I love you, Daniel. You're a pain in my ass and I *do* want to punch you in the throat sometimes, but God help me, I love you."

Daniel slowly closed his eyes and grinned. I started to say something, but he placed a finger over my lips.

"Shhh, I'm soaking up the fact that you said it first," he said and opened his eyes. They sparkled brighter than ever before. "You aren't going to try to run away or hurt me if I tell you that I love you too, are you?"

"Not today. Now can we get back to the kissing before someone barges in on us?"

"Absolutely," he purred as he pulled me tighter to his chest and covered my mouth with his.

Chapter 15
Daniel

I'd just started kissing Evie again when someone cleared his throat in the doorway. I was ready to give whoever the hell it was a piece of my mind until I saw it was Alex.

Mental note to self: when Evie and I finally get down to business, I'm going to take her far away from here where we won't be interrupted on the regular.

"We have our orders," Alex said, nodding for us to follow him down the hall and into the conference room with everyone else.

As we walked into the room, the first thing I saw was Lana pacing along the back wall, chewing on the end of her thumbnail. I'd thought she had headed back to her house, but apparently not.

"No one will like this assignment," she said to a woman I'd never seen before, most likely her handler.

I'd heard Lana was a psychic, but I'd never really given it much thought because it wasn't that uncommon in our line of work; even I knew that. But the way she was looking at Evelyn had me worried. I wasn't sure how far into the future she could see or even if she had any control of that, but whatever she'd seen obviously didn't sit well. The other woman wrapped her arms around her, and Lana buried her face in her shoulder.

"Everyone have a seat please," Alex said when we were all in the room. "You all know Lana and her handler, Maria. They are here to relay very specific orders from corporate, and some of you are not going to be thrilled about them, not in the least." His eyes flickered to Tony and me. Suddenly I got a horrible feeling in the pit of my stomach. Tony seemed to notice because he sat up a little straighter and glanced in my direction. No, we weren't gonna be thrilled one bit, and we could both feel it.

"Evelyn, Josephine, you're going to escort our…*guest*, back to the hotel and procure a room. Reservations have already been made under a pseudonym," he said.

"Alone? Hell no!" Tony shouted. He slapped the table and stood up so fast that he knocked his chair over.

I nodded vehemently in agreement. Boss-man Alex was on crack if he thought this was going to happen.

"This is not up for discussion, gentleman," he responded firmly. "Evelyn and Josephine are more than capable of handling themselves out there, and both of you know that. They're what this Mzetir is looking for: young, prime breeding-age women. They can slip in without raising much suspicion. The rest of us will be in a safe house just outside the perimeter, ready for rescue if need be."

I suddenly felt like I couldn't breathe, like there was something squatting on the middle of my chest, holding me down. Alex still rambled on about the assignment, and I probably should have been listening. But all I could think about was Evie going out there without *me* at her side.

After the meeting, everyone scattered to take care of what Ev called "pre-mission rituals." I wanted to go with her, but she said she needed a half-hour or so to do her "thing," so I snuck a quick kiss when no one was looking before she headed down the hall; her cheeks colored a soft pink. God, how I loved that I did that to her; it made me want to grab her and drag her into a corner to see where else she blushed.

Turned out everyone's "thing" was different, and I hadn't been doing this long enough to have come up with my own.

Z worked the bag in the training room like a maniac and refused to talk to anyone. He wouldn't even let me in to use any of the other equipment. *Asshat.*

I tried meditating in the bedroom instead, and that seemed effective — until Tony and Josie stumbled in with half their clothes already off and promptly kicked me out. Big surprise that was their "thing." Of course, in the grand scheme of "things," that's one I could totally get on board with.

I made my way down the hall, intent on killing the rest of my time away from Evie in the weapons room, bugging Chris, but as I passed by the girls' bedroom, I heard the shower running.

Evelyn.

Stopping in front of the door, I laid my palms and forehead against the painted wood and could feel her on the other side; her unique energy flowed right through the plywood. I argued with myself as I reached down and gripped the knob.

Do I do this? Do I blatantly invade her space and interrupt her pre-assignment ritual solely based on the fact that every cell in my body is screaming for me to open that door?

The doorknob turned, and I felt like I was outside my own body. It was as if I had no control over the weight of my palm pushing the door open or my feet as they carried me across the floor; all there was, right then, was the *need* to breathe the same air as her.

I stood in the middle of the room. The air inside was slightly thick, humid, a result of the bathroom door being open a crack. I could hear Evie talking to herself, but I couldn't make out the words. I could have moved closer and listened in, I suppose, but that felt intrusive.

Yeah, 'cause creeping into the middle of her bedroom while she's naked in the shower isn't weird at all.

"Who's out there?" she asked. I had been so busy standing there with my eyes closed, soaking up the Evelyn in the air, that I hadn't even heard her turn off the shower.

"It's me, Dan," I admitted, wishing I had ducked out the door and bolted downstairs as soon as the words left my mouth.

"Daniel…" she said with a sigh that was clearly born of frustration.

"Wait, before you say or think anything, just hear me out, okay?"

The bathroom door swung open, and she walked out wrapped in a giant white towel. "All right, that's reasonable."

My eyes took on a mind of their own and darted up and down her body four times. The only thing between me and total nirvana was one layer of terrycloth. I wondered how much sweet-talk it would take to get her out of that towel and into that bed against the wall.

"Uh…um…" I tried to form a coherent thought as all the blood in my body vacated my brain and headed south for the winter.

"This isn't a peep show, Daniel. Start talking," she said as she ducked into her closet to get dressed. At least now I was able to get a bead on my train of thought.

"Okay, so I know you told me it was your ritual to be alone and to wait for you, and I totally get that because I completely respect your pre-assignment 'thing,' but then Z kicked me out of the gym, Josie and Tony kicked me out of my own room, and I *swear* I was just passing by your room on my way downstairs to annoy Chris, and then it was like I had no control. I *had* to be in the same room with you. I had to be as close to you as I could without getting my ass kicked." I rambled like a lunatic and didn't recall taking a breath the entire time.

"And you thought lurking in my room while I was in the shower was okay?"

"No," I said defensively. "I tried staying in the hallway, but I couldn't. I had to—" *Don't say it out loud. You'll sound like a complete pussy* "—breathe the same air as you."

Pussy.

Evelyn stepped up in front of me and put her hands on my face, forcing me to look at her even though I felt like a complete idiot.

"It's okay." She kissed my lips gently. "I've been preparing for big assignments alone for over a hundred years, but today it just wasn't right. And then all of a sudden while I was in the shower, a sense of calm washed over me, and I knew you had to be near. It's weird, but I always know when you're close. It's like I can sense your energy, and it makes me feel…"

"Ten feet tall and bulletproof?"

"Yeah, exactly," she said, rubbing the tip of her nose against mine.

"I'm worried," I admitted, closing my eyes and nuzzling her neck, breathing her in deep. "What if—" I stopped. I didn't want to say it out loud, but I didn't know if I could *not* say it. I squeezed her tighter and kissed the skin behind her ear. "What if you don't come back?" I whispered. She rubbed my back and up into my hair, and instantly, the stress and panic about her going out alone subsided.

"Daniel, I've been doing this for quite some time, same with Jo. We'll be safe. Besides, this time I actually have something to come back to." She pressed her lips to my chest, and the sensation practically burned my skin through my T-shirt.

"I love you," I whispered and kissed the top of her head; her hair was still wet from the shower and smelled sweet.

"You know, I think I really like the way that sounds," she said with a wink as she raked her hands through her hair and whipped it into a quick braid. "I'm going to go meditate in the solarium. Do you want to come?"

"Yeah, I do."

Weaving her fingers between mine, we headed downstairs.

The meditation did wonders for the separation anxiety I'd been feeling, and it only came back slightly when Evelyn had to prepare for the mission with Josie.

While I paced the hall outside the magic room, I caught sight of the door that led to the subbasement. That beast, that infernal troll, was down there, and I was going to make sure he knew what was in for him if *any* harm came to Evie. My blood boiled in my veins as I stalked down the stairs, pushed through the mortuary doors and the hanging strips of industrial-strength plastic that hung in front of the holding cells. The unnatural vibe hanging in the air down there was practically visible, and it swirled the thickest around the third door. I peeked through the window and saw the creature crouched in the corner. Before I realized what I was doing, I'd flung open the door and had that stinky troll's face pinned to the rough brick wall of the cell.

"All right, you pathetic slab of otherworldly scum, I'm going to make this quick and perfectly clear," I said into his misshapen ear hole.

His breath blew back in my face. The putrid smell of death and Hell washed over me, and it was all I could do to keep from throwing up. In all fairness, that probably would have improved the smell.

The creature rattled something off in his born language; hell, it might in fact have been English and I was just too pissed for it to register. I fisted my hand in his greasy mane and clocked his head against the brick, leaving a smear of dark green troll blood on the stone.

"Shut the hell up and listen, you waste of space. If anything happens to Evelyn — and I mean *anything*— I'm holding you personally responsible. I will hunt you down, and by the time I'm through with you, there won't be enough pieces of you left to identify. Do I make myself clear?"

Apparently I'd struck a nerve because I was now standing in a puddle of troll piss.

"Feel better now, do we?" Alex asked as I walked out of the morgue.

"A little bit," I admitted, looking down at my urine-covered shoes.

"Good, but you'll need to burn those shoes. Troll emissions have a stench that is nearly impossible to get rid of." With an approving smile, he handed me a pair of boots and rubber gloves.

"How did you know I'd be down here?" I pulled on the gloves and removed my shoes, careful to not let anything touch my skin. "Are you gonna tell me that on top of running this place, being a hunter, and wielding a badass Divinity blade, you're a psychic too?"

"Hardly. I simply deduced what I would do were I in your situation and it was Isolde escorting our smelly friend back into the mouth of Hell. You remind me so much of myself, I'd wager that's why Gabriel sent you here," he mused out loud but mostly to himself.

"Gabriel…that was the name of the guy that recruited Chris and me," I said, thinking back to that day when a Lebriga rep knocked on my dorm room door.

"Then you are indeed something special. He doesn't often recruit personally, not anymore."

"Anymore? What is he, some high-up bigwig or something now?" I laughed.

"Something like that; he's the head of the corporation."

Then it hit me: *G.* Gabriel.

Nice going, dumb-ass. Way to know who your boss is.

"Holy shit," I muttered. "Wait, is that who trained you?"

"That's correct, very good."

We started walking through the range and up the stairs to the main basement.

"I remember when he first appeared to me, I thought I was hallucinating," Alex continued. "I was drunk, as I was more often than not back then; it was how I coped with my 'condition.' And when a man appeared in my home with great white wings and bright red and gold robes, it didn't even occur to me that he might be anything other than a drunken vision."

"Okay, see this was some other Gabriel, then. I mean, there has to be more than one, right? The guy that I talked to didn't have wings. He just looked like a regular guy in a suit."

"Times have changed, Daniel. If you asked Gabriel, I'm sure he'd say that wings and robes are passé and ostentatious. He much prefers the subtlety of a fine Italian suit these days."

"Hold up," I said, pinching the bridge of my nose. "Gimme two seconds to wrap my head around this…So, we're talking Gabriel… with wings…like *the* Gabriel…voice of God, sent-from-the-heavens-on-high Gabriel?"

"Yes, *the* Gabriel."

"And *the* Gabriel hunted *me* down to come and work for him? And then issues *me* a Divinity blade? I mean…I can't….me? It's just… seriously, man, I am no one special."

"Daniel…"

"And I swear—a lot. I say 'shit' and 'hell' and 'goddamn' and 'Jesus Christ'…Jesus Christ, I say 'Jesus Christ'! They don't want someone like me working for them."

"Daniel, calm down. I assure you that if you weren't supposed to be here, you wouldn't be here. One of the usual recruiters would have spoken with you, and you would still be plodding away in the desert." He took off his glasses and looked me square in the eyes. "Can you honestly tell me that you don't already know you are where you're supposed to be? That you didn't feel it in your gut, in your very soul the moment you stepped foot into this house or saw Evelyn for the first time?"

"No," I said, shaking my head. "I knew when I was in Nevada that I was in the wrong place. It wasn't anything that was said or done; I just knew that it wasn't where I was supposed to be. It never felt like home."

"My point precisely."

"So, help me out here. Are we, like, God's army or something like that?" I asked, feeling silly for even saying it—and even sillier that I'd never asked it before. When Gabriel had recruited Chris and me, neither of us had even questioned the greater theological implication of hunting demons. Fighting bad guys, having cool toys, and getting to live forever had been pretty much kick-ass enough for us to sign up. "'Cause if Gabriel is an angel and we're working for him and he's working for God…"

"No, we are hunters, and if I had to categorize us as anything, I'd say we were more…humanity's army. I know it seems like there are legions of us, but in truth, we are few and far between. For every one true hunter who's born, a compatible handler is born as well, and that only happens every ten to twenty years—sometimes half a century or more—which is one of the reasons we live as long as we do. It is the only angelical gift we are given; everything else is born talent or learned skill."

"Like our ability to fight and use magic?"

"Yes. We aren't born with the knowledge to perform magic or the skill to fight, but we have the ability to learn these things at a highly accelerated rate. However, our capacity to recognize and see demons and the like as they truly are, that is a gift we all possess at birth."

"Is this Mzetir, is he…ya know…the Devil?"

"It's not that easy, Daniel. God, Satan, Heaven, and Hell, they all exist but not in the context in which we are taught in church. Satan isn't sitting on a street corner waiting to gobble up someone's soul and drag them back to Hell. He's in everything and everyone, as is God. Heaven and Hell, they're here on Earth. Heaven is what you feel when you're with Evelyn and it feels like you are the only two people in the world, and Hell is what we have sitting in a cell behind the morgue. Our job as hunters is to preserve that moment of Heaven here on this plane of existence and send the bits of Hell back to where they came from."

"I think I get it. So, do you think Gabriel brought me here solely based on my compatibility with the team, or do you think he knew, ya know, that Evelyn and I would, ya know?"

"Fall in love?" Alex asked with a sly smirk.

"Yeah."

"The life of a hunter can be a very lonely one, and Gabriel…how should I put this…he likes to see that we all find our heaven."

I began to understand the scope of what it was to be Evie, a hunter knowing that in her lifetime she'd only *just* touched the surface of

Heaven in the last month, with me, and I'd be damned if I couldn't give her the whole experience when this was through. I knew, down to my last bubbling molecule, that Evelyn and I were meant to be, fated by the heavens themselves.

"Thanks, Alex."

"My pleasure. Now come, we need to ready the gear for the safe house."

CHAPTER 16
EVELYN

Josie and I powered down a large amount of Tess's latest edition of potion, and we headed down to the garage. We would be delivering the troll in the black van Jo hated, which didn't surprise me much. You couldn't bring a bottle of water into one of her favorite vehicles, let alone a pustule-encrusted troll.

Jo also tested her panic button, an electrode complete with LoJack capabilities, embedded in the skin just behind her ear. Alex and Tony tried to get me to have one of those things installed ages ago when Tony and Walter had created it, but it was a little too Big Brother for me. I liked the idea of being able to disappear without a trace, however feigned that might be — because I knew damned well that if the powers that be at Lebriga wanted to find me, they could do so, anywhere. Still, it was the principle of the issue.

As soon as we stepped into the garage, the stench of troll urine smacked us both in the face.

"Ugh, that thing better not have pissed on any of my cars," Josie said.

"Nah, just on Danny's shoes," Tony answered with a laugh.

"Shut up, man," Daniel grumbled as he shoved the creature into the van. Once the cargo was loaded and secure, he walked me to the passenger door. Sliding his fingers into my belt loops and pulling me close, he said, "Be careful."

I didn't want to go without him; it felt so strange now not to have him with me all the time. But orders were orders.

"I'm always careful," I reassured him.

"I know you are. Just be extra careful, for me?" He squeezed me tight and buried his nose in my hair. I wondered if he was having the same bad feeling about this as I was. I tried not to think too much about it because if it was anything seriously bad, Lana would have stepped up and stopped the whole mission, or at least tried to, I hope.

"I love you," he whispered, so soft, so sure, that I could feel the weight of the words even though they were barely audible.

"Love you." I stretched up onto my toes and kissed the curve of his jaw, right below his ear, before hopping up into the passenger seat.

Tony slapped the back of the van twice, and we had the all-clear to roll. Halfway to our destination, our cargo became highly agitated. He started banging around the back of the van, shouting trollian obscenities at us and moving so violently Josie was having a hard time keeping in one lane.

"Listen, shit stain," Jo yelled into the rearview mirror as she sped down the freeway, "don't make me pull this thing over and let my girl Ev bust a cap in your foul ass. She's been itching to shoot something, and honestly, we really don't need you alive."

"You're bluffing," the troll spat back, giving the back doors another good hard kick and causing the metal to squeal in protest.

"You don't even have to slow down, Jo," I said. "I can take him out through his right eyeball just fine from here." I turned around in my seat and took aim with my .45.

The beast growled; his curled lip bore his teeth up to their blood-red gums. I cocked my revolver and started to squeeze the trigger. He immediately settled back against the bare metal on the inside of the van, and that was the last we heard from our little friend for the remainder of the ride.

After Josie parked the van down a dark alley close to the W, we continued on foot. Once inside the force field, we could finally let go of our smelly prisoner and carry on with our mission. If all went well, he'd go on about his normal troll business and Josie and I would check into the hotel, begin the process of sealing off our room with magic, and pray no red flags would be raised. If not, and the beast raised any kind of alarm as soon as we turned him loose, we'd pop a shot into the back of his head and get the hell out of Dodge while the getting was good.

Josie and I let him go, and he immediately sank into the first murky doorway he came across, so we began walking toward the W—making that God-awful girlie cackle that you hear when women get together—and all seemed to be going exactly as planned.

Actually, everything seemed to be going a little *too* well for my liking. Life around the hotel was copasetic and blissfully benign for the part of town we were in. Self-involved, pretentious idiots yammered away on their various devices as per usual, but something seemed…off. By the time we arrived at the W's main entrance, I felt my hunter sense swirling in the pit of my stomach. In fact, I'd had the sense we were about to walk into something we might not walk out of ever since we'd left the house.

"Galaxy," Josie said quietly. The tone in her voice told me her instincts were kicking in as well. *Galaxy* was the one code word we used in the worst of situations, a definite signal to get out and get out now.

I nodded in agreement. Jo and I were skilled hunters and had fought our way out of some seriously sticky situations before, but we weren't stupid, so without another word, we made an immediate about-face.

As we took our leave of that dreadful place, we noticed that every person on the street was turned in our direction. Glaring like a mob of hungry, mindless zombies, they all moved around to box us in on the red carpet in front of the W. This was not going to be the easiest of escapes, but it wasn't impossible, not yet. Just then, the massive glass doors whooshed open behind us.

"Oh dear, I hope you ladies weren't planning on leaving."

"You just got here."

Neither one of us needed to turn around to know who those thin, eerily childlike voices belonged to. Before I could utter a single spell in our defense, a dingy gray claw clamped over my mouth and we were being dragged into the lobby of the W. I twisted against the grip, my teeth trying to gain any kind of purchase on the flesh covering it.

"Such rude behavior, don't you agree, Narhael?" the apparent male twin asked as he examined his hand. Clearly, Josie had attempted to take a bite out of the hand over her mouth as well.

"Indeed, Epanael. I expected something more from hunters of this quality," Narhael said, and she sniffed my hair. "Hmm…a bit old and musty for my liking, but I think Father will be most pleased. He has an affinity for the antique."

"I think this hair would look lovely on you, my sister," Epanael said, picking up a handful of Josie's silky blond locks and letting the strands fall through his fingers.

"Over my dead body," Josie spat.

"Of course, my dear," he replied. "That's quite the idea."

Suddenly, Thing One and Thing Two stopped where they were, transfixed by some unseen force. Their eyes closed and hands clasped between them as they raised their free palms to the ceiling in a trance. "Father is ready to receive you," they said in unison.

Screw that.

"*Veig 'em grest'nth, g'tihl ni'eth kard, vieg ot'ema krasp,*" I whispered, calling upon the spells of strength and light, but my tattoos didn't ignite, and I felt no magic course through me at all.

The female, Narhael, crowed wickedly and doubled over in demonic laughter as she pointed a gangly finger at me.

"It thinks it can conjure in here," she cackled. She danced over in her odd, half-human gait and leaned down in my face. "You have no power of invocation this deep into Father's territory, silly hunter. You're as helpless as a human infant."

I could feel the color drain from my face, and I couldn't seem to vocalize what I wanted to say. Everything in my world collapsed in on itself for a moment until I heard Josie screech and then saw her kicking at the two trolls dragging her toward the elevator. The sound of my partner—my friend, my sister—snapped me back into reality and put the fight back into my soul. I wasn't prepared to die without knowing what making love to Daniel felt like.

With a quick prayer that Lana was keeping psychic tabs on us, I broke away from one of the beasts holding me and battled for all I was worth. If those rat bastards wanted to take *our* asses, they were going to have to work for it.

We'd taken out three goblins and two of the trolls when I felt pain in the back of my head and my world went black.

When I came to, I'd been moved and had the distinct taste of blood in my mouth. I was in the middle of a large room, facing a massive set of windows overlooking the city. I glanced around and tried to get my bearings while the room pitched and swayed underneath me; those trolls had really rung my bell.

Instincts kicked in, and I took a mental inventory of everything I could see, hear, and smell. It took a good couple of moments before I realized I was tied to a chair and not alone in the room. Josie was bound to the white leather chair next to me; her right eye was nearly swollen shut and a chunk of her hair caked red with blood, and judging by how I felt at the moment, I was pretty sure I looked about the same. Then I noticed Jo was glaring across the room at a man lounging on a lavish horseshoe sofa, flanked by the twin hybrid freaks of nature.

He appeared to be human, ridiculously human. Too human. He wore a maroon three-piece suit cut to fit him like a second skin, complete with a crisp white shirt, narrow black tie, and a pocket watch tucked into his vest. His hair was straight, shoulder-length, and blacker than anything I'd ever seen. He was reed thin, and his color seemed slightly off, but he had a sadistically regal air about him.

"I apologize for the bondage, but you left us no choice," he crooned with otherworldly cadence. He removed his enormous sunglasses and stroked the bare skin of Narhael's head like he was caressing a pet. He looked at me, and the cold, deep obsidian of his eyes explained why he wore the shades; one look at those would be a dead giveaway of what he was beneath the surface of his human-ish flesh. "I am Mzetir, and you are?" he asked with a quirk of his sculpted brow.

"Go to hell," Josie spat, literally shooting a wad of bloody saliva in the direction of our "host," for lack of a better term.

"I've been, thank you. Dreadful place, really. I much prefer this place, thank you. Humans have a certain…*joie de vivre*," he said as he rose from the couch and smoothed out the trousers of his suit.

He pawed at his hair, skin, and clothing; clearly he enjoyed the luxuries the human world could grant him, the materialistic prick. He sauntered over to where we were, floating across the floor like an apparition, and sniffed the air around us.

"Mmm…yes, you do have quite a lovely bouquet, classic." He screwed up his face and shook his head. "No, that's not the proper word…" He sampled the air again, waving it into his face with his hand to draw in the aroma. "Vintage," he said, his smile turning into an unnatural curve as he nodded. "Yes, *vintage* is the word I was looking for."

His intense, demonic stare made my skin crawl as he circled Josie and me slowly, looking us up and down like a farmer inspecting a pair of milk cows for purchase. That couldn't be a good sign.

Epanael trotted over and sidled up next to Josie, pressing his boney cheek against hers. His green, pebbled tongue lashed out and slid across her temple, lapping at the coagulated blood.

"You are so decadent, I want to keep you for myself," he whispered.

"Epanael!" Mzetir hissed, gnashing his pointed teeth at the creature who shrinked away in fear.

The next thing I knew, Mzetir's hand flashed up and disappeared behind my head, wrapping around the base of my skull. It hurt like a son-of-a-bitch, and I tried not to let him see how much, but I couldn't hold back the hiss of pain as he probed at the laceration his goons had left in the back of my head. It felt like he was digging under my flesh, trying to weasel his fingers into my brain, and just when I thought I couldn't take the agony a second longer, he pulled his hand back. He marveled at the fresh blood running down the center of his palm and over his wrist, seeping into the white cuff of his shirt—my blood. With lithe, almost balletic movement, he leapt over to Jo and swiped the thumb of his other hand over the wound on her forehead, gathering a smear of her blood as well. He swathed the thick digit over his bottom lip for a moment then sucked the whole thing into his mouth.

"Ohhh…" he moaned, his eyes fluttering closed for a second as he focused on my blood, still wet and sticky on the back of his hand. His black, slime-covered tongue danced over the sanguine fluid. "Ahhh, I can taste the power that flows through your veins, the raw hunter tang within the blood itself." He looked euphoric as he sucked down every last trace of our blood on his hands, and the tone of his voice shifted into its unnatural intonation. "Yes, this makes me want to revert to my true form and rut the pair of you at the same time, wild and ravenous. Imagine the glorious children we will make," he mused, taking a moment to wipe a string of gray drool off his chin and apparently gather his composure.

"You're going to have to kill us first," I said. There was no way in hell I was letting any part of that thing's dick, humanoid or otherwise, anywhere near me.

He tossed his head back and laughed heartily. "Sweet hunter, you will submit," he said, stroking my cheek with the back of his hand. "You will cry in fear, you will beg for it to end, you will scream in pain, and yes, you will die." He leaned his head down between mine and Josie's and whispered as if sharing the most intimate of secrets: "Gestation is immediate for my spawn. I almost can't contain my excitement when I think about how our young will feast on your supple pink flesh in a mere two days—at most."

Jo gasped and her eyes flashed to mine, riddled with the fear and panic I knew she was trying so desperately to hide.

"It is the nature of our kind and quite the honor, really. The ultimate mother's sacrifice," Narhael said, wandering over next to me and stroking my hair like he was trying to calm a frightened child.

Mzetir nodded in agreement, then turned and walked toward the lounge area, removed his jacket, folded it neatly, and placed it on a round, oversized, black leather ottoman while he continued around the sofa. He pulled the watch out of his vest pocket and set it on a nearby table, followed by his tie and the vest itself. Pushing open the sheer silver drapes, he pressed a button on the wall next to one of the massive windows. The panes of glass slid open, and his clean white shirt fell off his shoulders and down his arms into a puddle on the floor at his feet. We watched the pale flesh of his back darken and turn a deep blackish green, and two leathery wings appeared and unfolded before our eyes with a disgustingly wet, sticky sound as they spread a good ten feet across.

"Take them to the breeding facility," he said, stretching to the ceiling a hand that morphed into a long-taloned claw. "The scent and taste of their blood is too much for me to remain in form, and I don't wish to impregnate them here." He took a deep breath of the fresh air coming through the open window, and a ripping sound echoed through the room.

"You do not wish to seed them here, Father, in private?" Narhael asked.

"No, insemination can be a messy business, and I just got your mother's blood out of the carpet," he answered, and with a roll of his neck, his shoulder-length black hair gave way to a pair of glossy, twisted horns. He turned his head and glanced over his shoulder at us. "I am a horny devil after all, and something as grand as defiling two great hunters deserves an audience. Don't you agree?" He flashed a sick, terrifying grin before he leapt from the open window and shot straight up over the building.

Christ on a crutch, Lana, I hope your psychic ass is picking this shit up.

CHAPTER 17
DANIEL

I hated the sinking feeling in my gut as I watched Evelyn disappear down the driveway with Josie and that goddamned troll. Something wasn't right. I sensed it in my bones.

"Come on, we need to get to the safe house and set up," Tony said, clapping me on the shoulder. I nodded, hoping that if I kept occupied it would somehow keep my mind off the enormous knot growing in my stomach. If things were going to go wrong, someone would have put a stop to it, wouldn't they?

"Lana says these need to go too," Chris said, holding out two massive duffle bags as we loaded the last of our gear into the white passenger van. Lana's handler, Maria, stood behind him with two more bags.

"What is this?" I asked, taking one and feeling the weight. Whatever was in there was heavy as all hell.

"Weapons and explosives, so we need to be careful with this one." He maneuvered around me and gingerly set his other bag inside the van.

"We? Man, seriously? You know you guys are handlers, right? This isn't your game, Hoss." Z laughed as he walked around from the driver's side.

"No, we *all* must be there," Lana said from the doorway. She was white as a sheet as she clung to the wall for support.

"*Dios mio!* I told you I'd come and get you in a second," Maria said and ran to her, delicately pulling Lana's arm around her shoulders and taking on the majority of her weight.

"I know," she said with a weak smile. "It is just—"

Her entire body stiffened and contorted painfully as Maria tried to hold her upright. Her eyes opened wide and glazed over, blank, as she stared into the distance. She didn't even take a breath, and just as fast as she had whipped into the trance, she was out of it.

"Tess. I need Tess, now," she croaked, sucking in air and reaching a trembling hand up into the mop of black hair on Maria's head, where she poked around until she pulled out a pen as Chris rushed past her to fetch Tess.

"Is it always like that?" I asked Tony as we watched Maria holding onto Lana. I'd never actually seen anyone have visions before, so I wasn't sure if that was a normal occurrence or not.

"No, I've seen her space out before, but I've never seen her do anything like this," he answered, looking increasingly worried.

"She just started doing this today. Usually her visions are very quiet, almost serene." Maria walked her over to a chair and helped her sit.

"I'm right here in the room. Do you not realize how demeaning it is to talk about someone as if they were not there?" Lana asked, catching her breath.

"We're sorry, *mija*," Maria said as she stroked her hair, "it won't happen again."

Tess ran into the room.

"Hey, you okay?" She kneeled by Lana's side. "Chris said you had some kind of fit and—Jesus, Lana, you look like shit."

"Charming as always, aren't you, Tessa? Now, you have something to write on, yes?"

"No, let me get something. I'll be right back." She jumped to her feet.

"We do not have time," Lana said as she caught Tess by the wrist and scribbled on her arm. "I need you to go into your shop and bring everything I write down—fast. And can someone bring me water, please?"

Tess took off like a shot, and Lana leaned back against the chair, still trying to get a full breath as Meg disappeared into her office and brought out a bottle of water. Isolde rushed in, shoving Finn out of her way and heading straight for Lana.

"What in God's name happened? Are your visions doing this to you?" she asked, clutching Lana's head to her chest.

"Yes. I've never had them like this. These hit me like sledge hammer, more vivid than any I have ever had, and then it is as though someone physically breaks the stream, tears it in half and pulls pieces of the vision with it. So all I see is a second or two of time." She stood on shaky legs and turned for the van. "We need to move. I'll fill you in on the way."

After we'd secured the weapons and crew into two vehicles, we headed out, and Lana continued to explain what she could gather from her visions. One thing she knew for certain was that the whole crew—all of the handlers and remaining hunters—needed to be together at the safe house.

She had a vision en route and two more within an hour after our arrival. With each attack, I drew closer and closer to the edge. Clearly something was wrong with the mission. Evelyn and Josie were in danger, and all we were doing was sitting around on our damned hands. I wasn't sure how much more of it I could take.

"So, why are we still here, exactly? Why aren't we busting through that bubble right now since something is obviously wrong?" I asked as I paced the floor and pulled my hair in frustration.

"It does not work that way," Lana said, rubbing her temples and directing Tess and Finn as they mixed up some kind of magic bomb for her. She had tried to brew the concoction herself but almost blew us all to Kingdom Come when a vision had slapped her out of nowhere. "Number one, we don't know if they are even *in* trouble, and number two, we cannot do anything until I have seen it."

"But if they weren't in trouble, then why are we all here armed to the goddamned teeth? I say we get off our asses and slay some demons," I said to Tony and Z, trying to rally the other hunters' instincts.

"Do you *want* Evelyn to die?" Lana shouted, leaping off the cot she'd been resting on and fisting my shirt in her hands, clinging to me not only for support but in clear desperation. "Because even though I don't know what exactly is going on, I know it is not good.

And if you storm the castle like some sort of Braveheart William Wallace, you might as well kiss Evelyn and Josephine goodbye. That is what you want?"

"What? No, I—"

"Then shut the fuck up and let me do my job!" The vein in her forehead pulsed, and her white-knuckled fists trembled against my shirt.

"I'm sorry, I'm just…" I covered her hands, trying to steady her and think of a word to describe what I felt, but I couldn't think of the right one. Luckily, I didn't have to.

"I know, I am afraid too. Evelyn and I have had our differences, but we have been through a lot together." She sniffed and finally crumpled against my chest. "I have not seen anything at all about her or Josephine, and that frightens me to dea—" Her words cut off as she seized, her entire body locking up and jerking in my arms.

"Maria! Isolde! Chris! Somebody do something!" I yelled, watching her gasp for air like a fish out of water.

Chris skidded around the corner and swept Lana up into his arms; easing to the floor, he cradled her so she wouldn't hurt herself. Alex and Isolde ran in just as Lana started to turn purple from lack of oxygen. Isolde ripped off her sweater and eased it under Lana's head as she knelt on the floor next to her. She leaned down, practically lying on the floor, gripped Lana's face, and pressed their foreheads together. Lana's body froze, and her breathing stopped altogether for ten of the longest seconds I'd ever lived through. When her breath returned, she and Isolde were breathing in tandem and talking at the same time, rambling in a garbled mess of words and sounds that didn't make any sense.

"Isolde is a psychic conductor. She's trying to tap into Lana's visions and stabilize them," Alex explained.

"Okay, so, what, like two radios trying to get onto the same frequency? Not to question your authority, but why didn't we do this before?" I asked.

"We tried to talk Lana into doing this before we left the main house, but she refused. She said it was too early and Isolde would know when the time was right."

"How will we know when they're on the same channel?" Tony asked, clearly as anxious as me about the whole thing.

"We'll know."

We watched the two women babble like a pair of holy rollers at one of those tent revivals speaking in tongues, until they suddenly gasped and went completely still. There was something about that gasp in particular that made the hair on the back of my neck stand on end and my gut twist in on itself. Tony reached over and gripped my forearm in anticipation of what we might hear when they finally spoke, if they were going to speak at all.

"They're being taken, dragged down the street to a big building; it looks like a hospital." Lana and Isolde spoke in stereo, gasping again as another wave of the vision hit. "It *is* a hospital, a breeding center."

"Jesus Christ," Tony said. His finger dug into my arm, but I was beyond feeling any pain at that point.

"Mzetir will impregnate them with his seed, and these hybrid creatures will be the cornerstone of the collapse of Lebriga."

"What of Josephine and Evelyn?" Alex asked, clearly trying to remain calm.

"They will die," Lana said quietly as she came out of the trance.

The sound of her words hadn't even completely died down when Alex's phone rang.

"Yes," he said as he listened to the voice on the other end of the phone. "Understood." He loosened his tie and scanned the room quickly. Everyone stood on edge, waiting for our plan of action. "Handlers, arm yourselves. This mission just escalated to Level Black."

One of the first things they taught you as a hunter was the two words you never wanted to hear associated with your mission: *Level Black*. Once a mission had reached that level, odds of coming out alive were seriously stacked against you.

Quietly and efficiently, hunter and handler alike jumped to attention, moving to arms like a well-oiled machine, as if we'd fought together every day of our lives. Weapons and ammunition flew through the air like a circus juggling act as Chris distributed them to his teammates, and I didn't even realize I hadn't moved an inch until Tony gave me a small shove to jolt me back into the moment.

"Hey man, are you up for this?" he asked tentatively. "This is some pretty heavy shit on your third assignment, to be asked to put your life on the line for a crew you barely know."

I looked up at him and tried to process what he'd just said. Everyone had stopped to hear what I would say; even Chris, who knew me better than anyone in the house, looked at me expectantly. Did they really think I'd bail out now, with Evelyn's life on the line?

"I'd give my life for every person in this room in a heartbeat, any day of the week and twice on Sunday," I said, and I picked up my Divinity blade and sliced a finger on the razor-sharp edge, bringing her to life.

Alex smiled and tipped his sword to me in a salute as he cracked the hilt against the wall and touched the vibrating weapon to his palm. Damn, he was cool.

While I strapped on my .45s and cartridge belt, Tess walked over and handed me Evie's blade, carefully wrapped in a leather casing.

"Here, you guys are going to need to give this to Ev. I know Lana hasn't seen if you'll get to her in time, but I also know if you show up to save her ass empty-handed, she'll hand you yours."

I thanked her and tucked the wrapped sword safely behind mine. "So what's in that stuff you and Finn are cooking up? Nitrogen? C4?"

She smiled up at me, and, for the first time since this mission had started, I saw something that soothed the twisting knot in my stomach.

"Hope."

CHAPTER 18
EVELYN

Josie and I stood in complete shock and disgust at the scene we'd just witnessed. In all my years as a hunter, I'd witnessed a number of creatures shed their human form in front of me but never an unveiling of that magnitude. The transition had been so fluid and effortless I knew we were dealing with one seriously nasty demon. Possibly the nastiest one any of us had ever seen in our lifetimes.

"I wish I could do that," Epanael sighed as he gazed wistfully out the window.

"What's the matter, wing envy? Or is it that you can't get it up like Daddy?" I asked, sarcasm dripping off of every word.

"You need to muzzle your pet, Sister, before I rip her tongue from her mouth and eat it as a snack," he snarled, ribbons of gray smoke curling off his body as the distinct scent of brimstone burned the inside of my nose.

"Oh, please try," I snarked, sticking my tongue out as far as I could and waving it at him.

Narhael leapt in front of Epanael and blocked him as he made a wild beeline for me. She held him at bay while his small teeth gnashed at my face over her shoulder, spraying his spittle across the room. Apparently, even demons didn't like their "manhood" put to question.

"She's trying to provoke you, fool," Narhael chastised, casting a glare in my direction while she shoved her brother away. She sauntered back across the room with a disturbingly sinister sweetness. She grinned innocently, leaning down and placing a hand on my belly. "The only thing keeping you alive right now is my sheer desire to listen to my brother and sister slowly devour you from the inside out, and when they've consumed every last ounce of your soft tissue and you are nothing but a shell, I'm going to relish every last drop of sweet marrow deep within every one of your bones," she whispered.

Loud, raucous belly laughter erupted out of me to the point where I almost felt I would pass out. I didn't know if it was fear, desperation, or simply the proverbial straw that broke the camel's back, but I couldn't stop laughing.

"I hope my middle finger gets lodged in your gullet and chokes you to death, you sick, evil, wannabe demon bitch," I said with every ounce of calm and certainty that I possessed at the moment.

"HA! Now that's what I'm talkin' 'bout," Josie cackled as the half-bred Hell spawns fumed, their flesh emitting foul-smelling smoke with their anger.

A large burly troll stepped in front of them, his head bowed and his eyes downcast in respect. "Forgive me, but we should move these hunters before—"

"Before they wind up dead. That *would* make Father most displeased," Narhael hissed with a twitch of her lip.

"Most displeased indeed," Epanael bristled next to her, nodding his agreement.

"Let's see how tough you are without your gun," a troll growled in my ear and hauled me to my feet, the very beast Josie and I had had in our custody that morning.

"You actually think I need my gun to kill you," I said with a reverse head butt so fast it knocked the creature off kilter enough to loosen his grip on me for a split second.

And a split second was all I needed. I gave him a hearty elbow to the gut, breaking his hold on me completely, and leapt onto his back as he doubled over. Swinging my bound wrists under his chin, I squeezed off his air supply.

The troll sputtered and tried to knock me off his back by slamming me up against a wall, but with my hands tied together, that only served to increase the strangulation. He fell to his knees, and out of the corner of my eye, I could see Josie doing her best to keep the other bastards engaged.

But, unfortunately, we were simply outnumbered, and right after our scuffle in the room, Jo and I found ourselves led through the lobby, paraded past the front desk like a pair of prized heifers on our way to meet the big bad bull. Every set of otherworldly creature eyeballs were on us. The males leered and licked their vile lips while the females looked envious of our predicament; I'm certain any one of them would have given their own young to be in our shoes. And as we passed, every beast bowed its head and uttered a variant of congratulations or praise for our great sacrifice. I wanted to be sick, and I could see Josie turning three shades of green.

"Don't you dare throw up. Don't give them the satisfaction," I said to her as we walked through the crowd.

She nodded and took a calming breath, and our escorts gave us each a hefty shove. The throng of onlookers erupted into a chorus of cheers at the violence, which only brought on another swift push through the sliding glass doors and out onto the sidewalk.

Josie and I froze.

"They're not coming," Josie said, blinking out at the complete and utter normalcy surrounding us.

As I quickly looked around, I saw she was right. There was no rescue in sight, not even a hint of anything remotely resembling panic amongst the general public strolling down the street. We were, for all intents and purposes, alone.

I thought about my last minutes at the house and how that precious moment had been with Daniel, feeling his arms wrapped around me and the warm press of his chest against my cheek. He had told me he loved me, and I could still hear his voice, clear as day. But it was becoming evident with every passing second that I would never hear him or feel his lips on mine ever again. The last thing I would know on this planet, this plane of miserable existence, was the sick, twisted touch of a sadistic beast.

Like hell.

Giving up just wasn't in my nature. I hadn't let the demons masquerading as doctors, nurses, and orderlies at Agnews break me a hundred years ago, and back then I hadn't even had dick to live for.

Now I had Tess, Alex, Isolde, and my whole crew, my whole family to live for. Now, I had Daniel.

"No," I growled, digging my heels in to get my boots to gain some kind of purchase on the concrete. Josie followed suit, snarling and spitting a string of obscenities *I'd* never even heard of, and I was a good fifty years older than her.

We bit and scratched, screamed and cursed every single inch we were dragged down the sidewalk, hoping and praying to garner some kind of acknowledgment from any of the "human" passersby. Not one single person even raised an eyebrow at two women being herded by a pack of trolls and two half-breeds. It was as if we were invisible to Mzetir's human zombies, but Jo and I dug in and didn't let that deter us for a second.

"Are you two going to continue this ridiculousness the entire way?" Narhael asked after a block.

"There really is no point," Epanael said while he moved in behind me so closely I had no choice but to move and walk at his pace. I felt something sharp against my lower back but couldn't recall seeing him with any kind of blade before. "I could throw you down in the street right here out in the open and fuck you dead, and no one would even blink a single eyeball," he whispered, and when I felt the same object jab against my back, it dawned on me that it wasn't a dagger or knife.

Gross.

His gangly hand slid around my neck and up over my chin, forcibly turning my head as his slimy tongue touched my skin. One of his fingers reached up to the corner of my mouth, brushing over my lips, and I took the opportunity I'd been given. I opened and bit hard, down to the bone. Epanael wailed and released me, and I whirled around, spitting his rancid blood back in his face. His uninjured hand flashed up and wrapped around my windpipe, hoisting me a foot above the ground and cutting off my airflow completely.

The world around me started to blur around the edges as unconsciousness crept up and threatened to overtake me. Spots of light bounced around in my field of vision, and I was just about out when an explosion rattled the ground and he dropped me. I pulled in deep breaths of air while green lightning crackled across the sky along the surface of the force field. The filmy bubble withered and began to shrink away as the lightning skittered over the barrier.

"What the hell was that?" one of the trolls asked.

Bone-chilling screams rang out in the distance, and I noticed the humans around us staring. One woman on the other side of the street stopped to take stock of her surroundings. It was as if she'd woken up from a dream and didn't quite know where she was. Her eyes swept the block and came to rest on Josie and me bound at the wrists and surrounded by at least half a dozen uncloaked trolls — not to mention the hideously disgusting Narhael and Epanael. Her mouth opened and closed as her pea brain appeared to process the scene she looked at.

"Back to the hotel!" Narhael screamed, and she picked me up with one hand and tossed me over her shoulder like a sack. Chunks of sidewalk whizzed by as we hurtled back to the W.

That's when the back of my neck started to burn, and I heard two voices loud and clear in amid the insanity.

"EVELYN!"

"JOSIE!"

The invisible force field had dissipated at a rapid rate. People came to, and I felt the magic within my body spark to life and pulse under my skin. The powers of the healing tattoo on my back kicked in, and I could almost feel the gaping wound on the back of my head closing. I had my magic again. But I wasn't certain for how long, so I took full advantage.

"Veig 'em grest'nth!" I conjured up the spell of strength, and I raised my hands and delivered a double-fisted kidney punch to Narhael's right side. She howled in pain but only slowed for half a step as she continued to run for the safety of the hotel.

I ramped up my magic again, preparing for a second strike. I'd keep attacking that spot until I went right through her flesh and pulled her damned kidney out with my bare hands if I had to. I'd only gotten half of the spell out when Narhael skidded to a stop and I heard Tony's voice, loud and clear.

"Hey, assholes, you wanna put my girlfriend and best friend down so I can kick your asses?"

Angling my head, I peered around Narhael's gangly body. Standing in the middle of the street between us and the W was our entire crew. Every hunter and handler stood at the ready for an attack of serious proportions.

Alex and Daniel tapped the ends of their swords on the asphalt, and the welcome, familiar hum of the Divinity blades filled the air like a song from Heaven. Then I saw the hilt of my blade sticking up out of the leather case strapped to Daniel's back, and I could feel her calling me to arms with her sisters.

Daniel pointed his sword at Narhael with a silent but highly deadly promise that he would come after her first.

"What is that?" one of the trolls asked, extending a shaky claw.

"Your ticket back to Hell, bitch," Josie spat.

"We'll see about that." Epanael smiled wickedly as he made odd clicking noises.

Trolls, demons, goblins, and some other creatures that I'd never seen before poured out of the surrounding buildings and into the street, ready to fight. My gut gurgled and knotted as Narhael lifted me off her shoulder and dropped me on my ass on the sidewalk. At that point, I couldn't tell if that was a good sign or bad, but one thing I knew for sure and felt with every molecule in my body was that if I was destined to die that day, at least it would be with Daniel.

Yes, that day was a good day to die.

CHAPTER 19
DANIEL

The time had come. The cavalry had arrived from the safe house, and we were ready to bring the pain to Mzetir's wicked world.

Once at the edge of his territory, Chris and I inserted detonators into the healthy brick of C4 while the entire crew stood back at a safe distance, and we placed the device in front of the force field. We then ran a length of wire from the small hunk of plastic explosives to the barrels of Tess's latest masterpiece...*Hope*. Fitting name for it, really, because I was chock full of hope. Hope that Evelyn was still alive, hope that I could keep her that way, hope that I didn't screw the entire mission up somehow, and hope that I didn't get anyone, including myself, killed...hope was my middle name right now. Daniel "Hope" Summers.

"You ready to do this, brother?" Chris asked, hooking up the last of the wires from the explosives to the charge box.

I stopped for a second and took a quick look around at my surroundings. The sky was clear, the air was sweet, I was about to go save my girl, and hopefully get to take out some serious bad guys in the process.

"Yeah, man, it's a good day to die."

"That it is, my brotha'. That it is," he said with a grin, then shouted, "Clear!" and flipped the switch on the detonator box.

The first charge blew a hole in the force field about the size of my head. It wasn't as big as I'd thought it would be, but it would be big enough to get the job done. With a second, smaller explosion, green smoke billowed out of the barrel, igniting the open edges of the barrier like wildfire. The bubble seemed to scream in pain as if it was living, breathing matter being eaten away. The distorted air dissipated right before our eyes, and that's when we knew Tess's concoction had worked.

Locked, loaded, and armed to the teeth, we made our way into Mzetir's territory like a plague of all that was goodness and light.

Humans wandering the streets became confused and out of sorts, while trolls and goblins skittered into buildings like cockroaches. Demons hissed in our direction as we passed but quickly scurried inside before we could get even remotely close.

As we approached an intersection east of the W, I saw Evelyn in the distance, slung over the shoulder of that female half-breed. She was only about a hundred yards away at the end of the street, and granted, I couldn't see her face, but I'd recognize that ass of hers anywhere. The male was next to them with what I assumed to be Josie and a slew of troll goons swirling around them all. The group stopped where they were, doing their damnedest to instill fear and stare us down. Fear was the last thing on any of our minds.

Alex and I drew our blades and called them to life as Tony rattled what I could only assume was a threat to the male twin. I honestly didn't know what he said because I was slightly preoccupied with deciding what part of that hybrid bitch's body I was going to lop off first.

The gangly, gross twins hoisted the girls and dropped them onto the ground as more otherworldly scum trickled out of the buildings and surrounded us like locusts descending on a crop. Z stepped up with a grin as he looked to Tony and me.

"I'll clear a path through the vermin, and you two get our girls the hell out of there." He slung his MK16 over his shoulder and ripped a pair of *Bagh nakh* daggers off of his belt as he eyed the encroaching beasts. "This is gonna be fun," he said, sliding his fingers through the handle grips and giving each blade a twirl.

Alex also gripped his blade and swiped and sliced at the creatures left in Z's wake, the two of them literally cutting a swath through the growing number of trolls, goblins, and the like. Tony pulled out his katana as I gripped the hilt of my blade, and we dove into the fray after them, fighting our way to Evelyn and Josie with every ounce of strength in our bodies.

The swarm of beasts swallowed the four of us fast. For every creature we killed, three more popped up in its place to claw and bite at us. I couldn't see Evie between the swirling mass of bodies, and I started to panic. The twins or any one of their cohorts could have been dragging her back to the hotel at that very moment and I'd never know it.

"Evelyn!" I shouted, trying to get my head above the mob. "Evelyn!" I sank my blade into a demon's belly and pushed his corpse aside, trying to desperately catch a glimpse of her; I needed to see that she was safe, or what I was doing had absolutely no point. The ground rumbled beneath my feet, and I heard Evie's voice boil up over the screaming sounds of chaos around me.

"G'tihl ni'eth kard kef oc b'crol!"

With a thundering crack and a flash of blinding light, a pathway erupted as creatures flew out of the way, blown back from the sheer force of the power she'd invoked. A gust of wind whooshed through the space between us, hitting me in the face with blast of pure Evelyn. Reaching over my shoulder, I pulled her sword off my back and hurled it in her direction. I watched in awe as she caught it with one hand, swept the scabbard off, sliced her palm to activate the ancient magic, and sank the metal into the belly of an approaching foe, all within the space of five seconds.

Damn, I loved her.

The smile on her face suddenly melted, though, and she ran toward me, her arms and legs pumping like mad as she bounded across the short distance, whispering another spell. She planted her right foot on the asphalt and leapt over my head like a gazelle, landing in front of the female hybrid that had been sneaking up behind me. Her sword sliced through the air in a blur, faster than my eyes could register what had happened, and a twitching demon limb landed in front of me.

"You will *never* lay a claw on him, or anyone else for that matter, ever again." The sun glinted off her silver blade as it circled around and swiped, lopping the head from the creature's body with one smooth stroke.

An ungodly shriek from across the street caught my attention, and I saw the male abomination's look of horror. Evidently he'd witnessed Evelyn decapitate his sister. He ran toward us at full speed, spewing obscenities and emitting a seriously foul-smelling kind of smoke. He must have had complete tunnel vision on Evie because he never even saw Jo, ready and waiting for him to step into her path Tony's katana clutched in her hands. With one fluid swipe of the Japanese blade, the hybrid's grotesque gray body crumpled to the ground, the forward momentum catapulting his head right next to where his sister's lay in the street. It was sickly surreal—emphasis, I suppose, on the "sick" part.

As if on cue, the remaining creatures pulled back up the boulevard and sought refuge inside the hotel where they might be protected by Mzetir's dark magic. We'd see what we could do about *that*.

Moving toward the center of that twisted corner of the universe, I took notice of how much damage we'd done. Then I saw the rest of the crew wading through the lifeless bodies of hellish beasts. We were all bruised and bleeding, but at least we were all still alive. Standing outside the W, we looked at the massive sliding glass doors and the madness teaming behind it.

"The energy coming off of this place is pure evil," Tess said with a shiver.

Isolde nodded in agreement. "Can you see the aura? I've never seen one so muddy and harsh in my life."

"Can't we just surround this shit-hole with c4 and blow it back to Hell?" Finn asked, wiping the sweat and goblin blood off his brow.

"Unfortunately, no. We would have no confirmation that Mzetir was, in fact, dead," Alex answered. "Gabriel's orders were very specific: we must ensure that Mzetir goes back to Hell, even if we have to escort him there ourselves."

"Gladly," Evelyn said as she straightened her shoulders, closed her eyes, and took a deep, cleansing breath. She raised her blade to her lips, whispering words of encouragement to her weapon before she reached over, grabbed me by the shirt, and pulled my mouth to hers. "For luck and, ya know, just in case," she said with a smile. "All right, let's deliver this motherfucker back to Hell in as many pieces as we can."

"Amen, sister," Josie agreed, strapping on a pair of katana blades.

"What's our plan of action, boss?" Tony asked Alex.

"Kill the beasts and save as many humans as we can."

"Just another day at the office, then," Z commented.

Tess, Isolde, and Maria stepped up onto the sidewalk in front of us and, with raised hands, blessed the crew with clarity, strength, and light. As they spoke, trolls, goblins, and demons seethed behind the glass, snarling and baring their teeth with the feigned bravery the interior of the hotel gave them.

When the ladies returned to the line, Alex raised his blade in the air, and Evelyn followed suit, touching the tip of her sword to his. As I moved mine into place, the metal connected with a surge of power and energy so raw it shot down my arm and rocked my entire body; I'd never felt so powerful in my life. I heard my own voice in perfect unison with Evie's and Alex's before I'd realized I was even speaking. They were words I'd never uttered in my life, and I had no idea how I knew them, but my mouth moved as if those were the only words I was capable of vocalizing.

"With the power of Divinity three, we unleash our wrath unto thee."

Electrically charged air washed over us as bolts of white light shot from the apex of our conjoined blades, shattering every window of the W.

Razor-sharp shards of glass rained down before our eyes and onto the concrete. It crunched under our feet as we moved forward through what was left of the sliding entrance doors and into the belly of the beast.

Demons launched themselves at us, and trolls and goblins surged forward in an all-out attack. Evelyn and I stuck with Alex, fighting our way through the lobby. The rest of the crew would have to take care of that mess; we had to find Mzetir, and we were all but certain he'd be up in his luxury suite, waiting out the heat of the battle in safety, the coward. We hit the stairwell with a vengeance, bounding up the steps two and three at once, not wanting to waste time with the elevator. I could feel my blade vibrating in my hand, pulsing with raw power as we moved closer and closer to Mzetir's lair.

"Just FYI, this guy changes forms wicked fast, so be prepared to walk in on anything," Evie said when we got to the top of the stairs.

We stood outside the door of the suite and glanced at each other. Wordless communication flickered between us, and, on a base level, I knew we were all ready to meet this beast and take him down. Alex kicked open the door to the suite, and a disembodied human head rolled across the room, coming to rest at our feet.

"Worthless prophets," Mzetir sneered in his human form, stepping over three decapitated corpses as he glared at me with his black, soul-sucking eyes. "Not a single one of them predicted Gabriel bringing you into the picture, young one. This is quite the inconvenience, to say the least. However, I do love fresh young hunter, especially with a nice habanero peach glaze and those fine little red potatoes." A black, barbed tongue slid across his lips. "But that's neither here nor there. We're reasonable…beings. I'm sure we can work out some kind of negotiation." He drummed the end of his fingers together in thought as he paced back and forth.

"There will be no negotiations," Alex corrected, but Mzetir continued.

"You robbed me of my minions and my young, but I've decided that I will let you live. I will crawl back into that ridiculous hole of a world I came from without a word if you allow me two of your female hunters for breeding."

"You will go back to Hell alone, and in pieces."

"I'm trying to be reasonable," Mzetir growled. His hands clenched into fists and opened into giant claws. "Your kind has ruled this miserable planet for thousands of years, and it's my turn!"

With a deep pull of air, the average-sized "man" before us grew in height and width. Two massive wings violently ripped from the flesh of his back, their shadow consuming every ounce of light in the room as the human face he wore split down the middle, slid off his skull, and plopped to the ground in two lifeless chunks. Alex and Evelyn stood absolutely still, steadfast and sure as they watched the horror unfold before them. On any other day, I'd have been petrified and about ready to shit down my leg, but not today. Today I wasn't just one—we were three.

Mzetir lunged, swiping at us with one of his massive claws, and howled in pain as his dark purple blood spurted across the clean white carpet. Our blades had flashed forward, slicing through his bicep and leaving three deep gashes the size of my head in their wake.

The movement had been so fast, as if the weapons themselves had felt the need to sink into the unholy flesh, to taste the foul meat underneath the greenish black skin. Divinity's powerful magic was flowing through our veins, bringing harmony to the three swords as they sang out and we slashed at the demon before us.

Light crackled from the ancient script engraved into each sword as we worked the spell of light, reciting the words in unison. A bright white glow rippled through the markings on our arms, creating a shockwave of luminescence from the three of us. Mzetir was stunned momentarily, but not long enough for us to strike him down. The walls of the suite rattled as he roared and surged forward, singling out only one of us this time—Alex.

The back of Mzetir's hand crashed into Alex's chest, knocking him across the room like a rag doll. Evie and I scrambled back to guard our leader as he bounced to his feet, shook off the cobwebs, and wiped a trickle of blood off the corner of his mouth.

"We need contact with each other. Link arms and let our Divinity markings touch," he said as Mzetir strode across the suite, a confident grin twisting his evil mouth. Standing in a line against the far wall of the suite, we linked and recited the incantation one more time:

"G'tihl ni'eth kard, vieg ot'ema krasp!"

The demon stumbled back with the force of our magic and became paralyzed as a tidal wave of light collided with his dark, sinister energy.

This was our chance to strike, and Alex wasted no time as he took off in a sprint toward Mzetir, sword swinging. He leapt from the back of a nearby couch, ran three steps along the wall, and launched himself at the creature, flipping and spinning in the air before his blade sank up to the hilt into Mzetir's heart. As usual, Evelyn was two steps behind, bounding over the coffee table and then sliding across the floor, jabbing her sword up into the vile demon heart. My feet moved beneath me before I'd even made the conscious decision to do anything. I was flying faster than I'd ever moved in my life, the Divinity blade clutched tightly in my hand, leading the way. I scaled a stray piece of furniture, rolled on my shoulder, and popped up in time to bury my sword into the beast's chest.

Our blades connected inside the demon's body, completing a circuit of pure, Divinity-charged power. Mzetir's eyes and mouth snapped open and he gasped, his limbs going rigid as our magic ate away at the evil in his soul and we spoke the last words he would ever hear:

"With these swords we damn you and send you back to Hell. May the pain of every innocent soul you've stolen come back on you tenfold, for all eternity."

With that, our blades turned in unison, ripping the black muscle of his soulless heart to tattered shreds. His limbs jerked and fell limp, and the dark glow of his eyes blinked out as the last bit of foul breath escaped his gaping mouth. We pulled our swords free, and nasty-smelling steam billowed out of the wounds.

"That's just disgusting," I groaned, covering my nose and mouth against the sour, acrid scent.

"Brimstone. These creatures are just riddled with it." Alex limped over and clapped me on the shoulder. "Well done, my boy, well done," he said and collapsed onto the floor, bright red blood saturating his trousers.

"You're hurt," Evie cried. She rushed over and tore open his right pant leg, where a six-inch gash laid open the flesh of his thigh.

"It's just a scratch. Isolde will have me right as rain in no time," he said with a strained smile.

Knowing we had to get his leg stable before we could move, Evie and I bandaged up his wound with several lengths of luxury bathroom towels. But as we worked, the elevator outside the room dinged. We took our stand in front of the couch where Alex was laid, our swords at the ready. We had no idea what was happening downstairs; our crew could have been slaughtered, and this could be any number of creatures or demons ready to spill out into the hall.

Fortunately, the door to the suite had been ripped off in our fight with Mzetir, so we had a good view of the elevator doors as they whooshed open. A tall man with long flowing hair and an Armani suit stepped off.

Gabriel.

He walked over to the demon corpse and gave it a good nudge with the toe of his fine Italian leather shoe. When he finally turned to us and spoke, his voice was so smooth and, well, angelic.

"We've been tracking Mzetir all over the world for centuries," he said as he surveyed the lifeless body. "He wreaked more havoc on more civilizations than I care to admit, and try as we might, we never had the right crew at the right time to pin him down long enough to rid the world of his insanity…until now."

"Sir," Alex said, trying to stand up.

Gabriel raised his hand, silencing Alex as he walked over to the couch. He carefully unwound the makeshift bandage and pressed his perfectly manicured hand to the bleeding wound. When he pulled back an instant later, Alex's leg was as it had been before—not a mark on it, not even a single drop of blood on his skin. It was truly amazing; I'd never seen anything like that in my life.

"Gabriel, I—" I turned around to marvel at him, to thank him for choosing me and bringing me to my new family, but he was already gone. "Where'd he go?"

I ran over to the window and stuck my head out, only half-expecting to see him flying off into the sunset, his great, white wings stretched to unimaginable lengths as he soared through the air.

"He does that constantly. He loves a grand entrance, but enjoys a swift escape even more," Alex explained as he stood.

"But I had so much I wanted to say to him," I said, looking at Evelyn. I wanted to thank him for bringing her into my life.

It's okay, Daniel, I already know, Gabriel's voice sounded inside my head.

"He knows." Alex winked, and bent down to pick up a bottle of single malt scotch off the floor. He scrounged up three glasses and poured us each several fingers. "Salute," he said with a nod to Evie and me as he raised his glass in the air and knocked back the swanky libation in one gulp.

He really was one smooth, badass dude.

CHAPTER 20
EVELYN

We loaded into the elevator and headed down to the lobby to check on the rest of the crew. Still unsure of what spectacle we might be walking into, we prepared ourselves for anything. When the doors opened, I laughed and shook my head at the scene before us.

Walter was sitting on one of the black leather couches that had been ripped to shreds, alternately sucking on his inhaler and taking swigs of vodka while trying to see through the broken lenses of his glasses. Lana and Maria were sprawled on the floor at his feet, speaking in a mixture of Ukrainian, Spanish, and broken English.

Chris and Finn were trying to calm down a furious Tessa covered from head to toe in putrid-smelling troll blood.

"I'm sorry, T," Finn said in an attempt to reason with her. "It was either shoot him or let him take your head off, and in my defense, I've never seen or even heard of a troll exploding like that."

"Well, next time let him take my head off. I'm going to smell like a dead goat for two weeks," she seethed, trying in vain to get the blood out of her hair.

Chris rubbed her back and said, "Baby, it's not that bad." He took a sniff of her head and coughed. "See, not so bad," he choked out.

Meg and Z were perched in the middle of fluff and empty pillows on what was left of the round white couch, passing a bottle of Patron between them.

Tony was sitting on the bar with Josie in his lap, holding onto her for dear life and wearing some kind of demon tail like a feather boa.

Isolde rushed over and peppered Alex's face with kisses. Clearly she'd been worried about her husband, and rightly so; I couldn't imagine having had to suffer through an entire battle like that, not knowing if Daniel was okay or not. That must have been sheer torture.

I brushed my fingers against the back of Daniel's hand, and it was the single most wonderful feeling in the world. "Hey, are you okay?" I murmured, looking up at him.

He nodded. "Yeah, I'm fan-fucking-tastic."

Gathering me up in his arms, he swept me back into a dip and kissed me for all he was worth. I could hear everyone clapping and whooping their approval, which seemed to encourage him to press his body closer to mine. His fingers touched the ink on the back of my neck, and our special magic zapped right through me.

"Hey, Alex?" Daniel asked when we finally came up for air.

"Yes," he answered with a chuckle.

"I know we're going to have to give our debriefing and stuff, but you were there and…well, is this anything we have to do right *now?*" Daniel still juggled me in that dangerously low dip. "I mean, we're done here, right?"

"Yes, Daniel, we're done for now," Alex said, and he tossed a set of car keys at him.

Daniel caught them with one hand and slung me over his shoulder with the other before he practically ran out of what used to be a set of sliding glass doors. Parked on the street in front of the hotel was that sweet 1969 El Camino he'd so coveted. I had no idea how in the hell it had gotten there, but flinging open its passenger door, Daniel didn't hesitate to plop me into the seat and run around to the driver's side, sliding behind the wheel. He turned the key, and the engine purred to life like a giant black cat.

"What in the hell is going on?" I asked, allowing a mischievous grin to tug at the corners of my mouth.

He leaned across the front seat and grabbed me by the back of the neck, pulling my lips to his for another breath-stealing kiss. I could feel the ink of my tattoo warming under his fingertip as he traced the lines of the Eye.

"I have a promise to keep," Daniel whispered, dragging his finger down my spine to the hidden ink on my lower back, reminding me with just a touch where he'd promised to start making love to me.

"Daniel…" I breathed.

"Yes."

"Drive fast."

His foot pressed the pedal to the floor as we hurdled down the street as fast as the car would carry us, the air inside it growing thick and heavy with all the energy that had built up between us over the last few weeks. Daniel sped through the streets of Los Angeles as if he'd grown up on them, and before I knew it, he was pulling into the driveway of one of our safe houses. He stomped on the brake and slammed the car into park.

"Wait," he hollered when I tried to open my door. He quickly hopped out and ran over to my side of the car.

Honestly, I'd thought I was over old-world acts such as chivalry at that point in my life. It was something that had been all the fashion between men and women back in my day, but I'd noticed a significant decrease in the formality of courting over the decades. Nonetheless, I blushed like an idiot when Daniel reached in and offered me his hand. Who'd have known I was still holding onto those hopeless romantic ideals deep down inside?

As I put my hand in his, he yanked me out of the car and swept me up into his arms again, sprinting across the yard as he headed for the house like a pack of demons were after us. Moving faster than I'd seen human hands move in a really long time, Daniel managed to unlock the door and get us inside without dropping me on my ass.

"Someone's eager," I cracked as he kicked the door closed.

"You have no idea," he said breathlessly, pushing me against the wall in the foyer and starting to kiss me. Soft, warm, and wet, his mouth was sheer perfection; there was no two ways about it.

Daniel pinned my arms over my head as he pressed his body into mine, firm and tight. He slowly dragged his fingertips down along my torso, gathering up the hem of my T-shirt and pulling it over my head. His thumb rested low on my left hip, swirling over a patch of purple ink. His eyes darted up to the same type of flower, forever painted on the skin of my right shoulder and halfway down my arm. With a confident smirk, he curled his finger into the waistband of my jeans and pulled it away from my body enough to see the design that continued down.

"Excellent," he whispered before he took my hand again and led me down the hallway and into the first bedroom we stumbled on.

Daniel guided me to the bed and stripped off his own shirt while I lay back against the pillows. The Divinity blade had left backlit markings etched into his skin; over time, the ancient script would remain in scar form even after everything else had faded, like mine. But by morning, his flesh would be back to its flawless perfection, without a single sign of Divinity's power anywhere.

I sat up on my elbows to take in his toned upper body. Magic rolled over every inch of him, as if he'd been marked from head to toe with illuminating ink. He looked exquisite, like he'd descended right from the peaks of Mount Olympus.

"You're so beautiful," I breathed.

"Hey, that's my line," he said, and he crawled up onto the foot of the bed, dropping a chaste kiss on my bare stomach. "God, you taste amazing," he murmured as the next kiss lingered over the swell of my breast.

Starting with the crook of my right elbow, where the first tattooed curl began, he moved over my skin, tracing the curves of the creeping plant lightly, lovingly with his fingertips. When he reached the apex of my shoulder, he turned me onto my stomach, unhooking my bra and following the tattoo across my back. Every touch was wrought with such adoration that I wanted to cry. He paused every so often to pepper a flower with kisses and slow, deliberate swipes of his tongue. As he reached the curve of my left hip, nibbling the purple-hued bloom there, he fluidly rolled me onto my back and stared at the place where the vine disappeared under the waistband of my pants.

He toyed with me, dipping his finger underneath, and just when I thought I couldn't take it for another second, he slowly worked the denim off my body. His fingertips fluttered over the last few lines of the tattoo snaking down my thigh, and he kissed from my neck down to my breast. Daniel traced the letters of the strength incantation there with his tongue, sweeping past the last accent mark as he wrapped his lips around the tightening bud and drew it into his mouth.

I could feel the heat radiating out of the magic in my blood, and the light in my skin burned brighter. I was reaching a nuclear state of arousal and could have easily taken control of the situation and had us grunting and sweating like a pair of horny, wild beasts in under a minute. In the ring and out in the field, I was in charge, I called the shots, and I was the one pushing him to his mental and physical capacity. But this, right here, was where he ruled; this was where he pushed me to *my* breaking point, and Heaven help me, I liked the feeling of being putty in his skilled hands, bending to his will and trembling at his every touch.

"I can feel your magic," he said as he gently parted my legs with his body. "I can feel it calling me, pulling me to you. It's not like anything I've ever felt before, with anyone." His body hovered over mine, and I was completely enveloped in pure Daniel.

He moved an errant strand of hair out of my face, and his lips fluttered along the curve of my jaw, up to my ear. "You are my heaven, Evie," he whispered.

"Yes," I heard my voice say as I raked my fingers through his hair and kissed up and down his neck, my teeth scraping against the Japanese symbol on his shoulder.

The magic flowed freely between our conjoined bodies, pulsing and ramping up the passion double, triple, quadruple-fold. Brilliant light exploded in the small dark room, and it seemed the ceiling had opened to reveal the pearly gates themselves.

Heaven, here we come.

Acknowledgments

I would like to thank Omnific Publishing for believing in me again and Elizabeth Harper for creating such a wonderful publishing family. To my amazing team of editors and artists, you make what I do look effortless and beautiful. Colleen Keough Wagner, my own personal epiphany maker, you get my weird brain, understand my babble, and help me make it the best weirdness and babble that it can possibly be. Traci Olsen, world's awesomest publicist ever, sometimes I think we share a brain, which is kind of scary but so freaking cool. Victoria Michaels, my Yoda, grand master V, you show me the ways of the Jedi and give me the powers of The Force with your support and knowledge; I couldn't have written a better mentor if I'd tried. To my sisters from other misters, Kim, Mindy and Lecia, you are my closest and dearest friends; even though you all live on the other side of the country, I feel your support and love as if you were right next door. And to my amazingly fabulous love monkeys, you make this all worth it—thank you for taking the time out of your lives to read my words.

About the Author

Patricia Leever is a wife, stay-at-home mom of four, and owner of one dog and one really old cat. On the average school day she runs about town like a lunatic picking up and dropping off kids and trying to find a moment of quiet to write down a word or two. She's a sci-fi geek that loves to dress up like a zombie and participate in the local zombie march down Main St. and laugh as much as possible; laughter frees the mind and heals the soul.

Live. Breathe. Write.

PatriciaLeever.wordpress.com

⋯→Young Adult←⋯→

Shades of Atlantis and *Ember* by Carol Oates
Breaking Point by Jess Bowen
Life, Liberty, and Pursuit by Susan Kaye Quinn
Embrace by Cherie Colyer
Destiny's Fire by Trisha Wolfe
Streamline by Jennifer Lane

⋯→Erotic Romance←⋯→

Becoming sage by Kasi Alexander
Saving sunni by Kasi & Reggie Alexander
The Winemaker's Dinner: Appetizers by Dr. Ivan Rusilko & Everly Drummond

⋯→Anthologies and Singles←⋯→

A Valentine Anthology including short stories by Alice Clayton, Jennifer DeLucy, Nicki Elson, Jessica McQuinn, Victoria Michaels, and Alison Oburia

It's Only Kinky the First Time by Kasi Alexander
Learning the Ropes by Kasi & Reggie Alexander
The Winemaker's Dinner: RSVP by Dr. Ivan Rusilko
The Winemaker's Dinner: No Reservations by Everly Drummond
Big Guns by Jessica McQuinn
Concessions by Robin DeJarnett
Starstruck by Lisa Sanchez
New Flame by BJ Thornton
Shackled by Debra Anastasia
Swim Recruit by Jennifer Lane
Sway by Nicki Elson
Full Speed Ahead by Susan Kaye Quinn
The Second Sunrise by Hannah Downing
The Summer Prince by Carol Oates
Whatever it Takes by Sarah M. Glover